Forever Beth

~

The Truth of it All

By:
Elizabeth Cook-Howard

Book Three
of the
Forever Beth Series

Elizabeth Cook – Howard is a fulltime professional in the social services field, wife and mother to four beautiful children. Born and raised in Queens New York she moved to the Lower Hudson Valley Region of New York to raise her family. Creating and writing mystery and love stories since her teens it wasn't until her early forties she decided to pen and self-publish her work, hence the *Forever Beth Series. Lost and Found, Our Love* and now *The Truth of it All.*

Dedication

This book is gratefully dedicated to my four beautiful children Quentin, Angelica, Joshua and Ashley. Each of you make me proud to be your mom every day since being blessed into this world.

My husband who continues to encourage the "Writing Thing"

The fantastic readers who say they are my fans but in reality I am yours. Each of you that shared your personal journey and could relate to the story I am truly humble,

And

Especially dedicated to the memory of my beautiful cousin Marcia whose candle wick was put out before the wax could even melt. Heaven's most stylish angel yet.

Acknowledgements

So many to thank.

My oldest sister "Cynthia Shirley Cook" My dad's Satin Doll. My rock and my strength. Love you for all you have done.

My baby sister Stephanie Ann Cook who has helped me tremendously during the writing of "The Truth Of It All" Sister Power All the Way!

To Ms. Hollywood herself -Margaret N. who named the Forever Beth Series without even realizing it. See I do listen, well most of the time!

And

My mother Patricia. Without you and of course a Mr. Frank G. my life would not be.

TABLE OF CONTENTS

One of the penalties of being a human being is other human beings.

Christopher Morley

Prologue:

Once knew a woman beautiful as the day, lost her life needlessly for feeling only shame. She cried, laugh then cried once again for this was her final day of her unrest.

She dressed not in her Sunday dress, hat nor shoes, only wore confusion, loss and the feeling of being unloved and used.

As she stood during her final seconds, she prayed to God and confessed her weakness. Struggling with how peace would be granted, her final outspoken words "Death is the only way for peace isn't it?"

From her words a decision made, a loud popping noise, a bang. The bullet meant for another finally ended her self-inflicted pain.

Chapter 01: Here Again

I stare at the television hoping to see anything other than another update on my health or the news of the century, Detective Kevin Walker with the NYPD slumming as a detective when all along a multimillionaire himself and sole heir to his grandfather's billion dollar empire. One reporter questioning the police department's background checks and confirming that higher ups knew who he was.

Cynthia and Kevin over the past few weeks done well keeping the TV channel on everything but the news and newspapers, not one seen in anyone's possession while visiting with me. It wasn't until yesterday that I was able to change the channel on the TV, changing to the local news. The only time really I was awake and Kevin getting some much needed sleep. I turn to look at my husband now sleep in a very uncomfortable chair. His long legs stretched across, one hand holding up his head the other lingering into the bassinet, touching our pride and joy's hand as they each sleep. I smile instantly. I

*hope his nap last longer than the usual twenty
minutes.*

*Already four in the morning and I find myself
restless and bored. I begin watching PBS – How to
Paint. Not really paying attention I turn and re focus
on my husband and our sweet bundle of joy. I fight
tears battling to come forth. It's been several weeks
since that day, many weeks here in this hospital. But
in a few hours we are heading finally home. Back to
comfort back to the one place I feel the safest.
Although not one word spoken by anyone regarding
that day, the pain and tears tell it all. JD breaking
down each time I recall him sitting with me. I
remember him saying* "I'm not a praying man but I
thank the heavens for your survival and for blessing
me with my first great grandchild". *Until a few days
ago too weak to speak all I could do was smile at JD
and lightly squeeze his hand.*

*My loving sister aged a bit through all this –
because of all this. Yesterday pointing out the grey
hairs I caused. It felt good to laugh with her again.
But the pain, I see it. Everyone being brave, not
saying a word. Adele and John too by my side.
Worried for me yes but my heartaches knowing their*

tears were and are more so for their grandson. I heard it in Adele's voice shortly after. Sitting with me, whispering in my ear, "My grandson loves you with all he has to give. Baby you can't leave him, he only just begun to live". *So much pain I've caused and the one person I seemed to hurt the most is the man whose made me the happiest I've ever been.*

Interrupting my pity party, Nurse Cathy enters. I immediately put my finger over my lips and point to Kevin. With a smile and nod she understands.

In a whisper He finally sleeps!

Smiling, yes hopefully he will get somewhat of a decent rest.

How are you feeling?

Great. No offense but I can't wait for my discharge later today.

No offense taken, you've been here almost five weeks now. But leaving here doesn't mean you're done healing, you will have several restrictions to adhere to.

Before I can respond, I hear Kevin's voice. Stretching both his arms and legs Oh she will adhere to each and every rule I assure you.

Nurse Cathy smiles at me

11

Kevin I didn't mean to wake you.

You didn't. And why are you up?

Couldn't sleep.

Mrs. Walker would you like something to help you sleep?

No.. No I'm fine. Plus a rare opportunity to see my husband sleep.

Presenting a bit embarrassed I'm going to leave you two. I'm right outside if you need anything.

Thank you *Kevin responds as he stands, stretches again and lays next to me. Pulling me closer into him we lay in each other's embrace. Kissing the top of my head while caressing my arm* I missed this...I missed having you in my arms.

I know the feeling Mr. Walker but knowing you were and are with me is enough to get me by until we get home. *Lifting myself up to look Kevin directly in his eyes* Which by the way I need you to promise me when we get home no fuss and you will rest.

Smiling Me rest? You need to promise me you will take an easy.... Bed rest only, nothing more.

We will see. But right now *resuming my position but snuggling closer*, it feels good to be in your arms.

I'm going to take advantage of this before our beautiful bundle of joy wakes.

****

I open my eyes to a darkened living room. Refusing to go straight to bed when arriving home this afternoon I haggled with my husband to stay on the couch for about an hour, promising to let him know when I was ready to go up. In turn he would not make a fuss over me. Seeing how I am wrapped in blanket after blanket, I won the battle but the war seems to be something else.

I make my way to the main hallway and notice a glimmer of light coming from the kitchen. Entering I'm immediately mesmerized by the most beautiful sight. My husband shirtless and holding our precious gem against his chest. Swaying back and forth to the sounds of the Temptations singing Silent Night. With head tucked under Kevin's neck, the two sway with the beat of the music. Kevin's voice joins and my knees begin to weaken. I close my eyes and for a moment I'm taken back to our honeymoon where my man sang directly to me. A smile emerges upon my face. Involuntarily my body begins to sway to the beat. Feeling heat near my mouth I open my eyes to Kevin greeting my lips with a warm kiss. How good it feels.

In a whisper What are you doing up?

Taking in this beautiful scene.

You should be resting.

I just did and I have been over the past few weeks. Besides when I woke and didn't see the two of you, well.. .

No worries sweetheart, our daughter wanted her mom but I persuaded her to hang with me for a bit.

Persuade? *Questioning in a disbelief tone. I smile at the insinuation because I know the truth. Amanda Rose Walker is already daddy's little girl from the moment she made her appearance into this world.* Persuade hardly. Where is everyone?

Mrs. Clarke and Cynthia are hopefully enjoying front row seats at the Garden.

The Garden?

Knicks game then dinner at Sylvia's uptown. Tomorrow they will be driven upstate to the Culinary Institute for a cooking class, staying overnight and returning Sunday evening. Adele and John are home in their new condo only a few miles away and grandfather had to fly back to Houston.

Kevin did you put everyone out? *Inquiring in a displeased tone*

No *flashing that devilish smile* I just arranged everyone's schedule a bit. I wanted us to be alone. I want you and my daughter all to myself for the first few days of you both being home.

No one put up a fight?

No, everyone understood. However since arriving home your sister and Mrs. Clarke called three times, Adele called twice to insure I fed Amanda and JD, well he called once but had several items delivered.

Baby thank you.

Thank me? *Sighing* I should be thanking you *Tears developing in his eyes* You just don't know how much....

Knowing where this conversation is going I interrupt So shirtless, did our daughter share her dinner with you?

Clearing his throat of the muffle that was developing Something like that. I made the awful mistake of giving her a bottle then shortly after spinning her a bit.

The lesson learned?

After I feed her I should hand her back to you.

Funny Mr. Walker... very funny.

Pulling a chair out from the table for me to sit Are you hungry?

No not now.

Beth, you've been home for several hours. You didn't eat anything before leaving the hospital and you haven't had anything since being home.

I will but later.

Almost time for your medicine, you should coat your stomach with something first.

Kevin, no fuss remember! I'm fine.

Expressing a suppressed pissed look Okay Beth... Okay.

What did JD have delivered?

When you go up you will see.

Kevin?

You will see *handing me several pills and a glass of water.*

Picking through the seven pills I take five and place the other two to the side.

What are you doing?

Kevin?

The other two?

I want to sleep on my own.

You haven't been, you need the rest.

Trying to suppress the tears fighting to fall and desperately trying not to come off bitchy I attempt to explain without going into detail Kevin I don't like the feeling that's all. I just woke from a nap. Please let's not debate this.

I know what you're trying to avoid. You need to sleep, cat naps aren't enough.

Kevin...... *trying to restrain the frustration building* let's get Amanda ready for bed.

Trying to restrain his own frustration, I'm helped from my seat and escorted up to our bedroom.

Entering the nursery I'm in complete awe. A bit superstitious I refused to finish the nursery until our little one made his or her appearance. Further not finding out the sex the final touches would be specific and from what I see specific is an understatement.

Kevin you did this?

No I wish I could take credit. This is all JD.

When.... How?

I was just as blown away when I came up earlier today.

17

Opening the closet designer dresses and baby shoes. Anything one could imagine for a baby. Her closet looks more like a department store display showing only top brands. Her crib draped in pink and white silk? Written on the wall behind the crib, "Princess Amanda". The adjoining walls a mural of Princess Amanda's Kingdom. Oh Kevin this is too much.

No, it's just right! Come sit here for a second.

Taking a seat on the plush sofa I look down at my precious gem who is now asleep in my arms. Eternally I thank my heavenly father once again for my blessing.

Kevin returns with a small box Beth shortly after you told me you were having our baby I purchased this.

Shaking the box What is it?

Taking Amanda from my arms Open it and find out.

Opening the box the waterfall begins. Kevin it is beautiful *pulling out a diamond encrusted charm that reads Mom.* Thank you …

No, thank you for her *kissing Amanda.*

Wow already pushed to the backseat.

Never!

Could you fasten it please *Putting the necklace on*

There it looks beautiful on you.

Looking down at it again Mom.... Who knew me, a mom!

Me!

Kevin.... *Sighing*..... I hope I can live up to the title.

Baby you already are.

What time is it?

About six, why?

Give JD a call.

You go ahead. I'm going to prepare us some dinner and we are going to eat with no refusal.

Yes Sir Mr. Walker *and I laugh.*

Chapter 02: Two Steps Forward One Foot Back

I wake once again from one of my now frequent naps that replaces any type of extended sleep, waking to a sun filled empty room. Kevin not too far away I assume based on the tray housed with tea and toast on my night stand. I look over at the clock, already two in the afternoon and most of the day gone. Getting out of bed I'm not surprised by the empty bassinet. Wherever Kevin is I'm sure she is snuggled comfortably in his arms. I put on my robe to begin my hunt but my search is short lived. Before I even leave my bedroom Kevin returns with Amanda exactly in the place I said she would be. An automatic smile surfaces.

Hey you're awake.

I am..... *Taking Amanda into my arms* Hi beautiful... Are you hungry?

I just gave her a bottle. Besides you need to get showered, someone is coming by to see you in about twenty minutes.

Who?

You will see.

Kevin I'm not up to visitors right now.

For this person you are *Kevin's tone turning from asking to telling*

Who?

Christopher Kane

Pure annoyance overcomes my tone What - why?

I called him

Kevin, why? I didn't ask you to call him or anyone else!

Beth it is either talking to Christopher today or *Interrupting* Or what?

Look this isn't a debate. You cleaning the refrigerator at 2 in the morning is one thing, not sleeping another but the nightmares when you finally do close your eyes..... Beth this morning was the worst yet.

You could've just woke me up. This is bullshit Kevin.

I tried, but you wouldn't wake up.

Listen I don't need to talk to anyone right now okay!

Avoiding any type of eye contact with me You do and you will. Christopher will be here soon. You can meet him dressed or in what you are wearing right now but either way you will be meeting with him-today!

Taken back by the tone I check my own and attempt to soften my presentation with hopes of him leaving the matter alone It's too soon to meet with him.

Really? I recall meeting with Christopher immediately being one of the stipulations of your discharge and you agreeing.

Whatever *said with eye rolling and all*

Grabbing my hand and looking me directly in my eyes, no longer avoiding eye to eye contact You can be as pissed as you want. Your daughter needs all of you, well rested and healthy. I need you the same. *With a kiss on my forehead I'm released.*

Whatever Kevin

****

Beth how are you?

I'm actually fine.

Fine? Tell me what "fine" means to you?

I'm okay..... I'm here...

I'm here, what does that mean?

Exactly how it sounds

Kevin says you're having difficulty sleeping?

My husband worries needlessly

Maybe so but is his concern valid?

I sleep.

Many changes in the past month

Interrupting and I'm taking each of them in stride.

Each one? What are these changes?

My husband being outed – his whole life dissected in and by the media. My being in the hospital again

Interrupting In the hospital again?

I would rather not play this game

Presenting with a non-entertained look I assure you no game. You were in the hospital again? Why?

To give birth to my child!

And that's your reason for being in the hospital "again" *emphasis on the "again"*

You know what I mean

No I don't, please tell me why you were in the hospital again?

Trying to choose the right words I pause. The only rational answer I could come up with Because

Because?

Because my heart failed me!

Your heart failed you?

23

Yes

How did your heart fail you?

Pacing back and forth It stop working! Look it's a Sunday and I'm sure you have better things to do!

No I don't. How did your heart fail you?

It stopped working and because of that I almost killed my daughter.

Beth, your heart didn't fail you. Your heart could not handle the amount of stress you were under

Laughing... Yup that's it. I'm fixed now

Were you broken?

My voice gives into the emotion that was being held at the back of my throat. I am broken....... I'm not the same.

Tell me the difference

Five weeks ago I was the happiest I've ever been in my whole life. I had a husband who treated me as though I was his Goddess. We were expecting and so excited to be. I no longer felt that emptiness, the hole in my life. I finally felt content – complete. Then it happens.

Tell me, what happened?

Laughing with tears falling A woman who felt I took everything from her killed herself.

Just like that. Nothing more nothing less?

....

She killed herself in your presence?

Stifling my tears Yes

Killing herself in front of you was her initial plan?

Shaking my head No!

What was her plan as you know it to be?

In a whispering cry To kill me, to kill my baby.

And the nightmares?

I relive that moment each time I close my eyes....
Crying harder Her words, her telling me I could have prevented all of this.

Do you feel you could have prevented what had happened?

I don't know... Possibly not seeing her that day? Having security with me when talking to her? I don't know.

How do you think she meant it?

I don't know.... I don't understand any of it. She hated me based on what Michael fed her and what Karen told her. But knowing me for who I was did not change how she felt about me.

Beth you know as I know, our mind when at our weakest can be our own worst enemy. It sounds as though the truth as she believed was the core of her problems. Regardless how hard professionally we try to help resolve, if not given the truth to work with our efforts are in vein.

He told her all those things, twisted events to make them his own.

Who is he?

Michael! ..... He presented me to her as though I ruined his life *releasing a nervous like laugh* I ruined his life, really!

And that is his truth regardless how accurate or inaccurate he presents it. You can't change his perception, what he believes to be the truth as he knows it.

And he goes unpunished?

Unpunished for what?

For this *clutching my chest* for what happened to me for Angela taking her own life. He is responsible for Rosa and Rosie's death. He did all of it. He is responsible for all of it.

Beth..... He may have provided false information but he did not hold you hostage and he - Michael did not pull the trigger. He did not kill Rosie and Rosa.

No you're correct, he didn't pull the trigger himself. But he certainly supplied the ammunition. *Raising my voice* I know without his lies Karen would be alive, Angela would be alive and I wouldn't be here, in this moment having this fucking conversation with you. *Sobbing* Rosie and Rosa would be alive.

That may be but we have to deal with the present to have a future.

And just let the past be whatever it was, no accountability nor responsibility?

Yes.

Sarcastically For me to move on I have to overcome and move forward, ha then my life shall forever be fucked up!

Beth...

Chris I know you're a Christian and I apologize for my tone but this is absolute bullshit. *Raising my voice* Tell me how I'm able to close my eyes and sleep longer than fifteen minutes. You tell me how I will be able to give my all, all of me to my daughter and husband. *Tears run faster down my face* Tell me how I will be able to trust someone when they ask for help.... Tell me! The thought of even going to the

27

center scares the shit out of me and not because I'm afraid it will happen again but feeling Angela's presence, being in the place where I failed her.

All appropriate feelings Beth. You have a right and a need to mourn her death as well. In time you will have the confidence to face what you need to give you closure.

My response shielded by a sorrowful laugh Four years undergrad and two years in graduate school. A fucking licensed certified social worker and in an instant I became what I have been trained to help. Wonderful.

Beth it will take time, you have to give yourself some time to adjust to it all.

Time is something not promised.

Beth nothing in this world is promised.

A promise free world where the expectation is to forgive and forget and move on. Is that how you see it?

Dismissing my comment Beth a small assignment. Each time your thoughts circulates around this matter write it down, everything. Don't over think it just document what is on your mind at that time and when we meet again we will review.

Exhaling ... Alright I guess.

We can meet again on Wednesday, I will come back here.

I don't want you going out your way.

Standing Not going out my way. So you will document all!

Yes I will, thank you for taking the hike up here.

My pleasure. Now would it be possible to meet the new edition?

Of course. *Opening the door to my office I call for Kevin.* Wherever her dad is I'm sure she is....*And sure as shit, Amanda is in Kevin's arms.* Chris Wanted to meet Amanda.

Amanda?

Yes Amanda Rose.

Chris smiles. He knows the significance of her name. Beautiful name for a beautiful girl.

Thank you.

Alright Beth - Kevin enjoy the rest of your weekend and Beth I will see you on Wednesday. Call me if you want to talk before.

I will. Thanks again.

Beth *Kevin placing Amanda into my arms.* I'm going to walk Christopher to his car.

Puzzled Alright.... Thanks again..... See you soon Chris.

After approximately fifteen minutes Kevin joins myself, Amanda and Mrs. Clarke in the kitchen. With Mrs. Clarke back normalcy seems to be creeping back in.

Beth it looks as if she grown some since Friday.

She has a healthy appetite like her dad.

I wish her mother had more of an appetite *Kevin says in a sarcastic disapproved tone.*

Beth you haven't been eating?

Not eating - nor sleeping!

Mrs. Clarke my husband exaggerates *flashing a "shut up look" to Kevin!*

Shoot all the laser beams you want at me. If you're not going to listen to me then hopefully Mrs. Clarke will be the voice of reason.

Ignoring Kevin... Did you and Cynthia enjoy your weekend?

We sure did. Beth I did not know your sister was such a Knicks fan. I swear Patrick Ewing heard her when she questioned his foul shot abilities.

You were that close? *Looking now at Kevin.*

Close enough to reach out and touch someone.

Wow Mr. Walker.....

What about the Culinary Institute?

Loved it. It was a beautiful drive. We made coco Von, paired wines and ate. Wonderful trip. How was your first few days home?

With my daughter and husband, perfect. But I'm hoping since you are back he will have someone else to fuss over *looking at Kevin who is shaking his head as though not happy with my statement* Alright time to give my bundle of joy a bath.

Beth would you like some assistance?

No I have it Mrs. Clarke but thank you.

Okay, diner will be ready in an hour.

No rush...

As I make my way upstairs the phone rings

Beth you have a call.

Kevin tell Cynthia I will call her back...

Not Cynthia pickup upstairs.

Rushing now to my bedroom I pick up the phone

Hello

Baby girl how are you?

Hearing JD's voice I smile immediately I'm fine now that I'm talking to you. JD how are you?

No concerns here, I'm doing just fine. The better question is how are you?

I'm doing just fine *I hear the sounds of a very busy background,* JD where are you?

I'm in Nigeria but flying out to Newfoundland in a few minutes. I have a brief layover.

Oh please be safe. Any plans to stop in NY on your way home?

I have a better idea, for the Holidays I would love it if you, Kevin and my Amanda Rose spent the Holidays at our Lake Tahoe home.

Lake Tahoe?

Yes, you will have all the snow you want, a guaranteed white Christmas.

JD I don't do Holidays away from home.

You wouldn't be, you will be in your own home.

JD I don't know...

I'm not taking no for an answer. I already set things up with Kevin

I should have figured that.

Sugar I have to go now. I will see you and my beautiful great granddaughter next week.

Okay JD... Travel safe and I love you.

And I love you *his voice cracking.*

By the time I end my call Kevin has prepared Amanda's bath and about to undress her. Mr. Walker Lake Tahoe?

Yes Lake Tahoe.

Was this your idea?

Not really. Grandfather and I discussed getting out of the city for the Holidays and he thought Lake Tahoe would be the perfect place.

But what about Adele and John, will they be okay not spending the holidays with you?

Without me yes, without Amanda *smiling* no.

Then what do we do?

John, Adele, Cynthia and Mrs. Clarke will all spend the Holidays in Lake Tahoe.

Cynthia can't go, my nephews...

Your nephews will be spending Christmas with us as well but have plans in New York for New Years.

Amanda now undressed Kevin I don't know

No excuses. All is in place.

Just like that?

Just like that! We leave on Wednesday and beginning Saturday our family will begin to arrive. Now can we please bathe our daughter! *And just like that matter closed.*

****

Beth turn to me and look me in the eyes. You could have stopped him a long time ago. Why didn't you?

How?

You know how but instead you choose not to.

Crying uncontrollably I really don't know what I could have done.

Screaming Look at me

No please I'm so sorry

Look at me

No please don't make me

Screaming even louder Look at me, look at what you did.

Being shaken forcibly Beth wake up... Beth wake up.

Startled a bit I'm okay..... *Rolling into Kevin's arms.* I'm okay... *And I wipe away tears that managed to escape*

Pulling me closer to him Hey do you know your daughter has your beautiful eyes.

I said I'm okay

I didn't ask you anything. She has your Alaskan malamute - husky eyes.

Kevin!

She does

You know she will endure all those mean kids asking if she is normal.

Seeming alarmed What?

You know kids can be cruel.

If any little son of a bitch teases my daughter they and their parents will have to deal with me!

Mr. Walker *laughing* your daughter will be fine. From five to thirteen she will be teased for having mixed matched eyes. From thirteen on she will be complemented and often attracting young men.

Beth I don't want to hear this.

I recall shortly after meeting a certain gentleman he too complimented me on my eye color differences. Well I think they were compliments.

Baby they were but my daughter

Seeing and hearing the uneasiness I laugh harder Oh Mr. Walker.

Changing the subject Beth you and Amanda will need proper attire for Lake Tahoe

Kevin, it is cold I got that... *Smiling*

I must have the one woman in the world who hates to shop.

Shopping isn't the issue *well that too* it's where you want me to shop.

Ignoring my reply Anyway, I hired a private shopper who will be by later today.

Kevin I need to do Christmas shopping myself.

And we will once we arrive and settle in. However you and Amanda need proper clothing for travel and the first few days.

Not liking this I know I have no choice based on Dr. Monroe's Instructions of bed rest for the first week. I'm surprised Kevin agreed to Lake Tahoe. Alright Mr. Walker I'm at your beckoning call.

Don't Beth

Smiling don't what?

Rolling me over and climbing on top Don't say words that get me going.

You know I miss this

I miss it too. But what I missed more was you in my arms.

Kevin..... What happen to us just before

Pulling himself up Beth try to get a bit more sleep. It's four in the morning and I told grandfather I would join him on a conference call with the Nigerian office.

Kevin?

Kissing me get some rest. If Amanda wakes, I'll come back up for her

Kevin?

Sleep.

Just like that question ignored, matter dismissed and Kevin out the door. I turn on the TV and begin watching Green Acres. Although one of my favorite TV shows I must have seen this episode at least twenty times if not more. I pull out Terry's McMillians latest and begin reading and continue to do so until Kevin returns a bit after six

You are one hardheaded woman

And why do we say that?

Did you even try to go back to sleep?

I wasn't tired, besides I've been waiting to read this *holding up my book.* How did your conference call go?

It went.

My husband, CEO

Hmm not yet. Change of power doesn't happen until the end of January.

Well not only did you make local but national news yesterday.

Yes, vultures.

Kevin?

I'm going to shower then I have a call with Charles.

I haven't seen Charles, Thomas nor Donaldson since the incident Is everything okay?

Going over our travel agenda and security from this point on.

Immediately concerned for the need I panic Kevin security? Why?

Because anyone not living under a rock now knows who I am, who you and Amanda are.

And I am very sorry for that.

Turning to me Sorry? Baby it was eventually going to come out. You have nothing to apologize for.

But you're worried?

Not worried, concerned.

Well for this holiday we remain plain ole Mr. and Mrs. Walker low keyed and simple. No need to rush the craziness.

Smiling, low keyed and simple.... You've never been and never will be.

Hmmm....

Hugging me now hmmm what?

Not a thing Mr. Walker and if you keep me in your embrace a second more I will not only be taking a shower with you but reenacting our honeymoon.

Well as you can see I'm alert and ready but not until we are cleared.

Party pooper!

I'm smacked lightly on the ass Oh I can't wait Mrs. Walker.... I can not wait!

Chapter 03: Lake Tahoe Holiday

After about a six hour flight and forty – five minute drive we pull up to an amazing chalet home that sits perfectly on a snow covered mountain.

I must really love you Mr. Walker!

With a confused look Why is that?

California, hell the west coast was never on my bucket list. You know earthquakes and all.

Laughing No worries. Come on, let's get you and Mandy inside.

Stepping inside once again I'm surprised. I assumed Just another piece of property with no substance but I'm completely wrong. Walking through the doors immediately feels like home. We are greeted by an older white woman who seemed to know who we were.

Mr. And Mrs. Walker I'm Crystal Summers I'm one of the caretakers.

Hi Crystal nice to meet you. This is Mrs. Clarke.

The two exchange pleasantries

Mr. Walker your grandfather phoned and requested you phone him when you arrived.

Thank you. Were you able to setup the nursery?

Just as you requested Mr. Walker. If you like I can give you a tour now?

Beth I need to call grandfather back. Ms. Summers Could you give my wife and Mrs. Clarke the tour?

Certainly. This way.

Up another grand stairwell, Mrs. Clarke is shown her personal suite complete with sauna and a tub the size of pool. I smile at the thought of how Mr. Walker treats the women in his life. Passing five more bedrooms all with in suite amenities we arrive to the grand master suite.

Here you are Mrs. Walker and all the changes Mr. Walker requested have been completed.

What changes?

Come this way. *I follow*

Mr. Walker requested the addition of a nursery.

When Crystal opened the double doors I'm completely blown away. This man will do anything for his baby girl. This is absolutely stunning and you did this all with a few days notice?

Your husband was pretty specific and I might add has great taste.

41

He sure does. Mrs. Clarke did you know about this?

Not at all.

Wow!

Mrs. Walker the nursery isn't the only change made.

Frowning What else?

Walking over to the closet, even before the door opens I already know what to expect.

We expanded the closet a bit.

Questioning in my head why, the door opens and just as expected. From snow gear to gowns - anything a woman would want or need is seen. My newly introduced closet again resembles an upscale department store display. Mrs. Clarke I'm going to kill him...

Baby don't fault him for wanting you to have the best, you deserve it. You enjoy it as he enjoys providing it to you.

Yes Mrs. Clarke I will *feeling like a scolded child.*

So did everything get done to your liking Mrs. Walker?

To my liking? Really? Mr. Walker over the top but I love it all. *Kissing Kevin on the lips* Thank you!

Come Mandy let's see your room *and instantly Amanda is taken from my arms and now in the comfort hold of her dad.*

Can I show you the lower level?

Oh please do *and Mrs. Clarke and I follow.*

After completing my tour I return upstairs to the nursery where I find Kevin sitting in a rocker with Amanda in his arms. The sounds of Israel Kamakawiwo'ole singing Over The Rainbow filling the room. Kevin joining, singing directly to the first love of his life. Mesmerized just like her mom Amanda stares directly up at her dad. I can only imagine myself at her age feeling completely safe, serene and in the hold of my father. No movement at all from my little girl, just her bright eyes staring up at the greatest man in our world. I close my eyes and listen to every word.

Somewhere over the rainbow
Way up high
And the dreams that you dream of once in a
lullaby

Somewhere over the rainbow
Bluebirds fly
And the dreams that you dream of
Dreams really do come true

Someday I wish upon a star
Wake up where the clouds are far behind me
Where trouble melts like lemon drops
High above the chimney top
That's where you'll find me

Somewhere over the rainbow
Bluebirds fly
And the dreams that you dare to
Oh why oh why can't I

As Kevin and Israel finish serenading my baby girl into a serene slumber, I wrap my arms around my husband and kiss his neck.

Do you know you make me weak in the knees every time I hear your beautiful voice?

Really?

Yes you do and I see she too becomes hypnotized not only by your voice but you as a whole.

Well I'm going to have to sing to my girls more often

Yes you do.

I'm a man whose been blessed not once in my life but twice.

Ditto my husband and I never thought you could look any sexier to me but when you have our daughter in your arms.......

Pulling me closer, I love you, never forget and always know that…

How could I, wherever you are I will be.

I'm going to hold you to that *kissing me gently on my lips.*

I know you will.

Tell you what, while Mandy sleeps you and I could go into town and start shopping. Would you be up to it?

All for it. Besides for my daughter's first Christmas only I will be picking out her presents.

Correction Mrs. Walker our emphasis on our daughter's first Christmas and we picking out presents.

Realizing who I'm talking to Maybe you need to stay back

Confused by my comment Why?

Why? She's barely a month old. Mr. Walker and I will be limiting your spending. You already spent enough on both of us and we've been here only a few hours.

Baby sorry to say, two people you will never get a final say on regarding my spending. Number one is you and mini you, number two.

Kevin..

Interrupted Not another word. I'll let Mrs. Clarke know we are heading out. I'll meet you downstairs.

As usual the deepened base in his voice turns me inside out. Only this man could turn me on in this manner. I smile at the thought of the soon to be possibilities.

****

Around 4 pm Kevin and I arrive back to the house to find Charles and Erickson waiting. Both presenting unsettled with a look of pressing concern.

Hey what are you guys doing here, kissing Erickson then Charles.

Didn't your husband tell you I'm part of the package now?

Turning from Erickson to Kevin... Huh?

Erickson left PD and is with Durand Holdings.

Surprised by this Wow really?

Without my partner wouldn't be the same.

Huh.... *Turning back to Kevin* And everyone is here for the Holidays?

Beth we will talk later *no longer in an upbeat mood* but yes a full detail is being put together while we are here.

I know more is going on but right now trying to get answers will be a waste of energy.

Baby I need to go over a few things. I'll be about an hour.

Am I being dismissed? Alright I'll go up and check on Amanda.

Wait.. Charles could you take Erickson down to the study? I'll be down in a minute to join the two of you.

As I'm walking up the stairs Kevin stops me midway. Beth I don't want you to worry about anything.

I'm not but I know something is going on.

Yes, since the media..... We've received several threats.

Threats? Like what - why?

We don't think it is anything but taking all precautions.

Kevin what is the issue?

The change in power to start. I'm about to become the CEO and President of one of the most powerful companies.

And

And the color of my skin, who I am. Who my mother was. Just a bunch of narrow minded bigots.

Kevin seriously?

I expected some resistance and I can handle it. But threats against my family I can't take anything lightly.

Kevin I don't want you worrying about us.

That will happen regardless. I just need you to know how important it is to have security with you at all times ok?

Yes, I do and I will. But don't worry about Amanda and me, focus on you. Really, piss off the assholes who rather not see you in this position by being better than the best. Matter a fact a proposition, you show them what your made of and I will happily spend a few of your dollars.

Laughing A few dollars? I expect you to get the best for you and my daughter so a few dollars won't do.

Mr. Walker take your time with the A-Team, Erickson being your Mr. T *laughing.* Amanda and I are better than okay and we have plenty to do. You do what you need to.

You know I love you Beth?

I absolutely do *and I kiss my husband hard.*

****

Our few days without family went by in a flash. Already Saturday afternoon and everyone expected will be arriving in about an hour. Excited to see everyone but very uneasy about the hovering that undoubtedly will occur especially from Cynthia. Our last conversation by phone ended with her of course telling me I was to do as I am told. She will probably have a fit once she sees the extent of the decorating I've done, but in my defense I did most of the pointing – gesturing. Kevin, Erickson, Charles and Mrs. Clarke did the actual work. Looking around at our handy work, the last room completed well minus the Christmas tree. But even without, the room looks as if it was a photograph from a post card – a Norman Rockwell piece even. The massive fireplace draped in fresh pine and pinecone garland and stockings for everyone. The fire magnifying the pine scent which fills the family room.

I look across and still my sight on my two most precious people stretched across the floor, in front of the fireplace. Kevin laying flat on his back and Amanda laying on top of her dad. Kevin splitting his time between his family and work, holding phone conferences at all hours of the night due to the time change seems to be getting a much needed nap in before the craziness begins. All that is missing is a family dog to complete this picture perfect scene but my Tiger and his chubby size fills in perfectly, sleeping too in the wingback chair near the fireplace. Not wanting to disturb any of them I quietly return to the kitchen to assist Mrs. Clarke with lunch.

Mrs. Clarke what can I assist with?

Beth I have this taken care of. Relax, try to get a nap in too.

I'm well rested *a tiny lie* what can I do to help?

*Mrs. Clarke trying to suppress a smil*e I baked a batch of cookies that need to be iced.

Don't worry Mrs. Clarke I won't mess with the actual food, I'll stick to the cookies. *We both laugh.*

As the two of us prepare for our family the phone rings I'll get it.. Hello?

Hi Beth

Christopher?

Yes how are you?

I'm fine. Did I forget to cancel my appointment?

No you did, I received your message. Beth I was calling to see what time we could meet? I can come by today if you like?

Today? *Presenting very confused* I'm still in Lake Tahoe for the holidays.

And I am as well.

What? *Befuddled* You are? Wait did Kevin *pausing for a moment* Can I call you back?

Yes?

Trying to suppress my instant anger Give me about fifteen minutes. *Slamming the phone down immediately wakes both Kevin and Amanda.*

Alarmed Beth what's wrong?

Trying to limit my anger, trying with the greatest restraint to choose the appropriate words I pause in place Kevin why is Christopher in Lake Tahoe?

Beth...

Raising my voice Why?

Why? *Walking toward me* Mrs. Clarke could you take Mandy upstairs?

Without hesitance and without any type of eye or verbal exchange Mrs. Clarke takes Amanda into her arms and disappears immediately.

Beth lower your voice no need to be this upset.

Elizabeth Cook-Howard

No reason? No reason! What the fu... What the hell are you doing?

What you should be doing!

I told you I'm fine. Shit, how many damn times do I have to repeat myself!

Fine..... fine? *Presenting more agitated* This bullshit is going to stop now. You're not fine. You can pussyfoot around if you want to but I'm not going to sit back and see you waste away right in front of me. You don't eat, you don't sleep and you won't take the fucking medication prescribed.

Through clenched teeth Kevin I Said I'm fine

Yes you say it, over and over again but the sight of you speaks something different. Since we arrived here I can count the meals you've eaten. Better yet the crumbs you've passed off as a meal and the fucking nightmares when you do finally fall asleep, I hear them I see the pool you wake up in.

I can take care of my damn self. *Raising my voice to a higher octave* I'm not a child.

Then God damn it do it, take care of yourself. *Slamming his fist on the counter.* Do it!

Trying to hold back my mixed tears of feeling hurt and how dare you, I storm out of the kitchen to the living room. Following me, Kevin refuses to let the matter be.

Beth when are you and Christopher meeting?

....

Fuck Beth when?

I have to call him back.

Then start dialing.... Please.

Why didn't you talk to me first?

I tried repeatedly Beth. You dismissed me each and every time so I took matters into my own hands.

....

You want me to call?

No longer able to keep from crying Kevin, *tears falling* I don't mean to be this way... I'm trying... For you, for our daughter I'm trying. I'm......

Softening his voice Stop trying for us and do for yourself. I kept my mouth shut for the past few days... But you're wasting away right in front of my eyes.

I'm okay. I am.

You put on a front for us and yourself.

Kevin......

Look I made him a sweet deal. I flew him and his family out, rented a house down the road and will insure he and his family have the vacation of a lifetime.

Shaking my head Kevin.....

Can you call him back now... Please?

Just as I pick up the phone to call Christopher back the doorbell rings. I put the phone back on the cradle.

Beth go up and call now. I'll take care of everyone until you're done.

Reverting back to my teenage years I stomp up the stairs making my views on this matter known.

I End my call with Christopher and now need to regroup. I sit on the edge of my bed trying my best to shake this... whatever this is. Internally I beg God for guidance and strength. Asking him to get me through the holidays. But in the midst of my begging session with God a knock on my bedroom door.

Come in

What's going on with you? *Kissing me on my cheek*

Hey Cynthia... How was the flight?

Fine.... So?

Cynthia I'm fine.. Why won't anyone take me at my word?

Because your word is shit if no meaning is behind it.

That quick, he got to you!

Start talking!

Cynthia....

Don't Cynthia me. And by the look on Kevin's face you've been giving him hell.

Ugh.... Give it a rest. Go see your niece.

Beth we are far from done... But I will see my Amanda.

Cynthia exits and Kevin enters. What the fuck.

Everything set?

Yes Kevin.

When?

Tomorrow at 10

Presenting annoyed He couldn't come today?

Rolling my eyes I did not want to see him today okay!

Sighing.... Elizabeth – Elizabeth!

Yep a name so nice you gotta say it twice.

Shaking his head Let's go down and start our holiday *taking my hand into his, I follow in tow.*

Chapter 04: Unsettled Peace

You could've stopped him and you didn't!

I couldn't...... I can't

Yes you could have and you can. He didn't do this to me you did.

Please tell me how... I'm so sorry. Please I beg you tell me what to do, what could I have done?

Turn around Beth. Look at me, look at what you made me do.

No I can't. Please forgive me, I'm sorry

Look at me

Yelling I can't... Don't do this please

Turn around and see what you made me do... Turn around

No.... No.... Please no...

Then I'll come to you.......

Yelling No no no please no

Beth wake up.... Beth wake up

....

Wake up now.....

I wake to water being sprinkled onto my face.
Startled What are you doing?

Kevin how long has this been going on? Beth get up.

Stop

Beth wake up *and now I'm being shaken*

You just poured water on me so I'm up ... *I open my eyes to a room full.* What's wrong?

Beth are you okay?

I am. Cynthia? Adel ? What time is it?

2:30 baby. Are you ok?

Adele I'm fine. Please everyone go back to bed. I'm fine.

Cynthia, gram go back to bed my calls are done.

Are you sure? *Adele presenting concerned*

I don't need a sitter. I'm fine, everyone please go back to bed. I'm fine..

Alright baby. *And Adele exchanges a look with Kevin then John who I just noticed is in the doorway.*

Beth get up, you need to change.

Trying to force a laugh, Cynthia I'm a big girl I can change my own clothes.

Look you're not talking to Kevin, get up.

Cynthia I'm fine.

No you certainly are not. If this is what Kevin was talking about, you're far from fine. You're drenched in sweat and waking you up *and there is that look I was hoping to never see from my sister again. The look that caused her newly sporting grays* Beth how long has this been going on?

Kevin not making eye contact with me pulls out a fresh gown and places it on the bed. Do you want me to run you a shower?

No... I wish you two stop making a fuss and go back to bed. Cynthia we will talk in the morning ok!

Kevin you have this?

I do Cynthia...

Well I guess I'm fuckin invisible huh....

Your mouth missy. *Cynthia kisses me on the forehead* Kevin call me if you need anything.

I will.

Cynthia exits and I go into the bathroom to change. Upon my return I find Kevin changing the sheets. I assist with no words or eye contact exchange. Once done I grab my Terry McMillian novel and head downstairs.

Where are you going?

I don't want to keep you up. I'm going down to read.

I'm up.... Get into bed and read here.

Returning I get back into bed and begin to read. Kevin sits on the side rubbing his hands together.

My husband you worry needlessly...

Beth no time for your so called humor.

Kevin I'm seeing Chris in a few hours. I'm fine... Look at me.

You need to see what I see and hear what Cynthia and my grandparents just witnessed. *Kevin sighs deeply* Beth this *waving his hands in the air* can't go on. You cannot continue to go through this.

Kevin will you at least lay down?

Laying back and putting me into his arms I begin reading and continue uninterrupted until the sun comes up. Kevin around four finally falling asleep, I release myself from his hold and head down to the kitchen to get breakfast started. To my surprise Cynthia, Adele and Mrs. Clarke are already sitting at the table having their morning coffee.

Hey good morning ladies. You three are up bright and early.

Did you get any sleep Beth?

I did Cynthia. *Sensing the continued concern* Ladies please do not worry about me...

Beth sit.

Adele?

Sit down. *Surprised by her authoritative tone I sit immediately.*

Beth sweetheart you are sitting among three women that lived and are living. Each of us experiencing some sort of tragedy that left an everlasting imprint upon us. Baby we understand the pain and hurt you are going through, the losses you have to come to terms with, we understand. But nothing comes close to what you endured. Baby we understand your need to get through this in your own way but we don't want you losing yourself in the process, not to give up.

Since the day my grandson told John and me about you we knew you were the one for him. After meeting you and especially hearing your journey, I understood why you and he are drawn to one another, the bond the two of you share.

Interrupting Adele

No listen to me. I can't sit back and just watch any longer, none of us can. You need to know you have more love at this table, in this house then you will ever realize. Baby we are family, you are my family and we need to take care of each other.

Listening to Adele words I begin to cry, tears trickling down my cheeks. I know each of you ladies love me as I you but

Beth no buts. I made mistakes in my life, especially not seeing the signs my own daughter presented. She isn't here now and I'm not going to sit back and watch you go down that road. I know your past hasn't been uneventful. I see who your supports are and who hasn't been present. None of business but I will say the love your sister has for you comes damn close to maternal love.

I look over at my sister who begins to cry.

Baby we just want to remind you that you have love and will always have love. And with love sometimes loss becomes a factor. Unfortunately a lot of loss you have encountered and that can't be changed but know you have family to help you through anything I mean anything. You have family and supports to lean on. We are here whenever you needs us any time any day.

Adel, Cynthia, Mrs. Clarke thank you. I never realized what I had until last May. *Turning to my sister,* you have always been to me what I sought after. And understand that I'm a better- stronger person as a result. Adele - Mrs. Clarke you two ladies I feel the love and the warmth of family. I do and I appreciate it. But.... what happened to me, what I'm going through I will overcome. I just need time, I need to do this my way at my pace.

Honey time you have! Our concern is how you fill that time. We want you to know you have us, you're not alone and we aren't going anywhere. You were and are a blessing to my grandson, to me and John. We began to live happier after you entered Kevin's life, he my grandson in finally happy.

And there it is, the root of their concern. Me harming myself. I can't help but to laugh out loud.
I promise I am nowhere near that place. See missing then was a will to continue with life. Today, this moment from the day I met Kevin I have a will.

And with that will you need someone professionally to talk to.

Sighing deeply I know Cynthia, I'm actually meeting with Christopher today. Kevin somehow convinced this man to spend his holiday with his family here in Lake Tahoe.

Amen to my brother in law. That's a start, now let's work on the eating and dare not say your fine

Smiling... I won't say it but I need you three to listen to me..... I will get through this. I don't want you worrying about me. I just need a little time to work all this out. Okay.... No more on the topic. Now can we get this holiday thing going? A very large tree is being delivered in about an hour.

Beth

No, not another word on this subject. Now let's talk Christmas menus.

****

Hey how did the session go?

It went okay. Kevin thank you for arranging it.

So you two will meet again when?

Tomorrow and probably inappropriate but I invited him and his family over on Christmas Eve.

Good.

You had the house decorated for his children?

Not a big deal.

Oh it is. All of it. *Lowering my head as if embarrassed – ashamed even* I could never repay you for all you have done and doing for me.

Shaking his head Repay... You just don't get it.

I do Kevin *changing the subject* So Amanda has been shifted from person to person, not seeing her crib or Bassinet once.

I think I had her once and not for a good five minutes.

Since JD's arrival this afternoon he and Amanda have been joined at the hip.

I never thought I would see the day my grandfather would blow off a meeting.

Huh?

He was to be on a business call with me. But less than five minutes into the call he announced his need to care for his new great-granddaughter and informed all parties that he supports any decision I make.

You are kidding me.

Beth, I never thought I would see the day. And when the call was done I found him feeding Mandy in the kitchen while talking to gram and Cynthia.

That little girl has both you and JD wrapped around her small precious baby finger.

Hmmm, her mother has the same affect!

Ha ha... I guess we should head back down.

Before you do, check behind the door.

For what *sounding uneasy*

Just do it... Please

Looking behind the door I pull a garment bag off the hook. Mr. Walker what did you do now?

Open it....

Opening the garment bag I pull out a beautiful black knee length dress with a plunging back. Kevin the dress is beautiful but..

But not a word. You and I are headed out for the evening.

With a house full of people?

Yup and Mandy is being left in very capable hands. So you have an hour to get ready. I have a few more calls and when I return you should be just about ready. Okay Mrs. Walker!

Ahh excuse me, what it takes you five minutes to get ready?

Five minutes to your forty-five to be exact!

****

Stepping out of the shower I look into the mirror and trace the hideous mark that stretches across my chest with my fingers. My eyes begin to swell and a weeping cry emerges. I try to hinder any memory of that day. Until this moment I did a damn good job of doing so during my waking hours. But right now wide awake I'm brought back to that exact moment. Weeping I Immediately put my hands over my mouth to stifle any sound. But I can't shake the images from that day. I see Angela and hear her words "Beth turn to me". *I feel tightening in my chest, I see only darkness. Will I ever get pass this? With my forever embodied memorial of that day reality sets in. This will be with me forever. I weep even more.*

Knock…. Knock…. Beth are you okay?

………

Beth?

I'm fine *all I am able to say*

Entering without warning I scramble to cover myself, to hide what I rather not see and certainly not wanting Kevin to see. But my swift actions not quick enough. Instantly grabbing my hands to stop my cover-up, Kevin undoes what I manage to cover. With no words spoken I shake my head in protest and lower my head. Tears streaming down my face Kevin in one swift move raises my head to look into my eyes and upon contact begins kissing my tears away very slowly. The affection increases the water flow. He continues, making his way down my chest kissing now the hideous healing scar. Immediately tensing and pulling away Kevin pulls me firmly back into him and now kissing me passionately on my mouth.

Pulling myself away from his embrace Kevin please stop.

Ignoring my words Kevin lifts me into his arms and carries me into the main part of the bedroom. Placing me onto my feet, I turn to walk away. My hand is grabbed and I turn back to him. Looking into his eyes he completely disrobes me and I stand bare and embarrassed. Starting at the top of my head I'm kissed ending at my healing wound. Kevin moves his fingers across, never taking his eyes off me. He then takes my hand and I'm guided to the full length mirror.

This...... this beautiful mark is as beautiful as this *touching my C-section scar.* Both of these imperfections brought life to me. This one brought our beautiful little girl into this world and this one *touching the area still healing from my open heart surgery* brought you back from death. I can't see anything beyond their natural pure beauty. Don't ever feel you need to cover yourself in my presence because baby from here *I'm kissed on my head* to here *my feet are kissed* is as beautiful this very moment as the day I laid in bed with you for the very first time. Now I'm going to check on our daughter and family. You get dressed so I can have a night out with my very beautiful wife.

With his last words lingering in the air I'm kissed on the forehead then left standing in complete awe. Looking in the mirror I try to see the beauty of it all but the image staring back at me remains unchanged, just a hideous reminder.

After about an hour or so of getting myself together I make my way down the stairs. One would think Halle Berry was making an entrance by the response. JD, John and Kevin all stand when I'm noticed. Kevin shines that ever so handsome smile that makes me quiver.

Beth you look absolutely beautiful.

Thanks Cynthia *giving a half smile*

My darling... darling girl you look stunning.

Thanks Adele....

Making my way to Kevin Mr. Walker ready?

Kissing me softly on the lips Oh baby I am *taking my hand into his. Turing to Adele and Cynthia* You have all the numbers. Call me immediately if

Interrupted by JD You two enjoy this evening. Nothing to worry about here.

Stepping out of the house I'm escorted to the limousine that awaits.

Really Mr. Walker?

This is your life now Mrs. Walker. Deal with it.

May I ask where we are going?

You could but you will have to wait and see.

Chapter 05: Back to what we had

Not waiting for a reply Kevin stands and reaches for my hand. As awkward as I am the voices in my head orders me to stay seated but my physical attraction for my man triumphs and I stand immediately, following him onto the dance floor. With one hand wrapped around my waist and the other holding my hand I follow his lead, slowly dancing to A Sunday kind of Love. Pulling me closer into him, I lay my head on Kevin's chest, close my eyes and take in the words of the song. Kevin lowers his head and snuggles into my hair, whispering "I can't wait to have your beautiful body all to me".

Looking up into Kevin's eyes I want, no I need you just the same but *shaking my head* I'm not the same.

Kissing me on the lips, no you're not. Baby you are more beautiful than ever before.

You know what I mean.

Oh I do but only you see what you see. I will always see the beauty of it all. You are beautiful inside and out.

This man. What more to say but take me now. I lay my head back on his chest, close my eyes and inhale deeply to ingest his scent. As the song ends Kevin kisses me once again then leads us back to our seats. As we sit and stare into each other's eyes a very tall blonde haired blue eyes model looking woman approaches the table.

Mr. Walker all is confirmed.

Thank you.

Can I get you and Mrs. Walker anything more?

No thank you

Well then enjoy the rest of your evening *and before Miss all legs struts away she flashes a large smile at me.*

Mr. Walker a friend?

Completely ignoring my question Can I have you tonight?

What?

Can I have you tonight - Can I make love to my wife? *Kevin's expression presenting both mischievous but yet serious.*

Do you need to ask? I need and want you just the same.

Smiling that ever sexy smile Kevin stands and holds his hand out for mine Come with me.

Following orders I stand and place my hand into Kevin's. Where are we going?

Ignoring yet another of my questions Kevin leads us through the lobby of the hotel to a set of elevators. Once aboard Kevin begins kissing the back of my neck. I turn to face him and my upper thigh is stroked while my neck is being nibbled on. Mr. Walker what are you up to?

Taking a brief break from turning me inside out just by his slow sweet breathing on my neck You will see *and just then the elevator door opens and we enter a candle lit suite right as we step off the elevator. The sound of Etta James filling the air.*

Kevin taking my hand into his once again brings me into him. We begin swaying to the sweet sound.

Baby I love you every second of the day. When you're not in my prescience I'm incomplete.

Stop.... *Tears forming in my eyes.*

You need to know you and Mandy are my life. You need to know living life didn't begin until I had you in my arms.

Mr. Walker not until you did I know what love was, what living is. You assume I've done something for you but really, you're my miracle. *With no verbal response, Kevin kisses me sensually but hard. I melt like a piece of chocolate left on a counter on a hot summer's day. I'm kissed to the mid of my back, my dress is unzipped and falls. I step out. I'm guided to chaise and I sit. Very slowly my pantyhose are taken off followed by my panties. Kevin kneels in front of me, pulls me into him and begins kissing me. I instantly turn into butter, impatiently waiting for him to take me over and over again. And in this moment my wish is granted.*

****

Baby how do you feel, all ok?

With a very large smile I'm better than okay. I feel fantastic but Mr. Walker you had all this planned?

I did. After so long I didn't think making love to you with a house full would be wise.

Cocky aren't we.... You assumed I would be a loud eager beaver *laughing at my own words.*

Laughing too... Baby not you, I was worried about me.

73

Well I hope I made up for all the waiting you had to do.

I guess we both made up for lost time.

Kevin what happen with us right before….. *The words just roll out my mouth. Realizing after the fact that this moment was not the right time to have this discussion. Damn it Beth!*

………

Shit this wasn't the right time…. Shit……….Kevin?

……….

Kevin I'm sorry I shouldn't have

Interrupted Beth I will never ever forgive myself for *sighing* I'm so sorry.

And due to my big fucking mouth the mood changes. The pain returns to Kevin's face with tears glossing his eyes Kevin please I don't want to see you upset over something I did.

With a perplexed expression You did?

Yes what I did, my actions. That day at the center Michael came by asking for help. I should have handled things differently and certainly not had any involvement with him.

Beth you didn't push my buttons nor did you push me away.

Raising to a sit up position then why didn't you come home?

Sighing Because Erickson and I *pausing* we had Michael under surveillance.

What? Why?

Certain things just didn't add up, beginning with the incident at the apartment building.

Why didn't you say something?

Beth it was only a hunch.... Then *putting his head down* the incident at the center.

Lifting Kevin's head and kissing his lips I love you baby. We can't change what happened but promise me we will never be apart like that again.

Baby I promise you. *Tears begin to roll down his cheeks* And through it all you wanted to make sure I knew you loved me and prayed I would be taken care of.

Remembering what I said in that moment my own tears begin to fall. In that moment I wanted three things. (1) our baby to live (2) my sister to know I loved her and grateful for everything she had ever done for me and (3) for you to get over it and live.

Get over it just like that?

Yes just like that.

Baby... The thought of losing you *Kevin pulls me into him and hugs me tightly*

Well you didn't. Your big mouth, sassy, often times clumsy – awkward, redheaded, freckled wife is here with you.

And I will never stop thanking God for giving you back to me.

Ok Mr. Walker *climbing on top* can you take me again?

Beth....

Is that a yes or do I need to take matters into my own hands? *Still miles away from that just recent mood, I do as I threatened taking seat directly onto his manhood. Round three of total bliss begins.*

Chapter 06: Family & Friends Is All It Takes

Hey Cynthia I have the dishes, you sit and enjoy the rest of the evening.

I am enjoying my evening besides it will only take a few minutes to knock this mess out of the way.

Joining Cynthia and me in the kitchen And I see where you get it from.

Mr. Walker are you saying something negative about the woman who raised me? *laughing*

Not at all. Just confirming that neither of you can just sit and enjoy the moment.

That isn't so

Oh he's right

Cynthia how can you leave me on the island all by myself?

Well if you think your on an island right now, hell yes I'm leaving you all by yourself.

The kitchen erupts into laughter.

What are we missing in here?

Not a thing, your grandson and my sister get a kick out of themselves.

Beth I must say this was one of the best Christmas's I've had in a long time.

I'm glad you enjoyed Adele. It looks like John enjoyed himself too.

Yes too much. Kevin why would you let that man talk you into a game of basketball?

Gram he asked me *laughing.* How could I deny him? Plus you heard the mess he was saying. But I have to admit he still has game.

He has game alright. When I need help getting that man in and out of bed you better be right by my side.

Responding from the family room Woman you do know I can hear you.

Good so I don't need to repeat myself. *Shaking her head* At your age playing some dang basketball. Something must be wrong with you.

But you heard your grandson loud and clear, I have game! This old man still got it.

John...... *Said in a jokingly displeased tone* Kevin did you hear from JD yet?

Yes he landed a few hours ago.

Sorry he couldn't stay the whole day but he said he was going to be here for his great – granddaughter's first Christmas and he was.

He seemed to have had a good time.

Beth it was a wonderful Christmas for all of us. We all enjoyed ourselves. Baby you did a fantastic job.

Yes you did Beth. It's been a long time *and Cynthia pauses* Just a great day.

My nephews seem to be enjoying themselves also.

I would too if I was catered to. Not lifting a damn finger.

Laughing at my sister Ms. Cook language

Cynthia responding with a very stern look And Kevin no more I mean it. They need to do some work. Hell they can shovel the snow.

We all laugh, even Cynthia at her own words.

I'm glad you all enjoyed.

Interrupted By Erickson who comes into the kitchen with a look of concern, my nephews appearing with him Hey Kevin could I talk to you a second?

Erickson everything okay?

Yeah, just a work related issue that requires Kevin's immediate attention *exchanging a look with Kevin.*

Okay.... Whatever you say *and Kevin and Erickson leave the kitchen. Turning to my nephews* I know you know something, spill!

A business call or something.

Really? You need to do better than that. If not I know my sister would love to hear about big booty Veronica.

Humph already heard.

Since you failed with the extortion attempt could you make us a couple of sandwiches?

No your aunt will not. When I'm done in here you can make your own sandwich and you better clean up after yourselves.

We feel the love ma, such love *and we all find ourselves once again laughing at Cynthia's reaction.*

I wonder what that is all about with Erickson?

Beth don't read into anything. Kevin is a busy man.

Hmm *responding to my sister's way of telling me not to start keep my mouth closed.*

And Erickson, he's starting to grow on me

Cynthia it took the first four years for me to understand that boy then - man now. *Laughing* when he would come down to Alabama it was like a scene from the Odd Couple. That boy would eat as though he had no home training and acted as f he was God's gift to women. He and Kevin lord two polar opposites. But one thing I know for sure, he and Kevin always had each other's back. When Kevin told me he left the force to work at Durand Holdings as his head security I was relieved.

Relieved?

Yes Relieved. With all that is going on, I felt you, Kevin and the baby would be well looked after.

Is she referring to the center incident or the threats?

But enough of this, I'm going to help your sister get this kitchen back in order then I'm going to plop myself next to John and enjoy the rest of this wonderful Christmas Day.

And with the three of us doing it, it will get done twice as fast.

Yes three *Mrs. Clarke placing Amanda in my arms* We three will take care of the kitchen and you and Amanda relax.

Baby girl you were sleep, what happened?

I think she woke up from hearing Kevin's voice.

Hey baby girl, okay you three you win. I'll check on Kevin then head up for a little one to one time with this exhausted one.

Walking towards the Office I hear Kevin's voice raised with anger. Not hearing any responses I assume he is on the phone. Just about to turn the knob, I hear the phone slam and The words "What the fuck is wrong with these fucking people". *I tap on the door and enter.*

Hey everything okay?

Startling Kevin, Beth it is. I'll be done in a few minutes.

Looking at Erickson he flashes that "Don't challenge him right now look. Please just do as he ask".

Okay I'm going to put Amanda back to sleep

Is she okay, why did she get up?

I think she heard her dad's voice

Softening his facial expression and voice I am so sorry baby. Bring her up and I will be right behind you.

Okay.... Hey Erickson called your "girlfriends" to wish them "all' a "Merry Christmas". *Trying to lighten the air.*

Laughing I did..... *shaking his head.*

Well the good news, my sister is beginning to like you. The bad news, well ask my nephews. *I close the door and head upstairs.*

Approximately thirty minutes later Kevin enters our bedroom with still that grim look. I know something is going on Mr. Walker.

All work baby. Nothing to worry about.

When you tell me don't worry that is when I begin to worry more for you. I don't like seeing you upset.

Flashing that gorgeous smile and caressing my face, Nothing to worry about. Now, I see my baby girl went back to sleep.

She tried to put up a fight.

Taking Amanda from my arms and placing her in her bassinet Well Mrs. Walker what would you like to do for the rest of this evening?

Would it be rude of us to light the fireplace here in the bedroom, turn on the TV and watch It's A Wonderful Life while laying in bed and sipping a glass of wine?

My grandparents are relaxing, Mrs. Clarke and Cynthia are watching a movie and your nephews are heading down to the hotel club. So I think spending the evening together alone will be the perfect ending to the second best Christmas I ever had.

Second curious to know what was the first?

Yes my second. My first was spent with my then beautiful fiancée last year.

This man really knows how to make me feel like I am truly his queen. Ditto, Mr. Walker…. Ditto!

Chapter 07: Facing Life Head On

Already after 11 pm, I sit in a very warm bath listening to Ray Charles singing "Ain't That Love". I close my eyes and give into the serene candle lit bathroom with the hint of jasmine in the air. Grateful to finally having a moment to myself I relive our recent holiday and how spectacular it was. I think back on New Year's and how Kevin surprised us all with a 12am Fireworks show and how he, my husband on our first anniversary - paper anniversary gave me a document acknowledging my rather large donation to Safe Haven, an international foundation that assist battered women and their children in Africa and South America. A cause I've only been able to minimally donate to over the years. *But of course he couldn't leave the gift giving just to that. I was also given a beautiful anklet with diamond shape hearts. An instant smile surfaces at the thought of Kevin knowing me so well. I think of our first night of love making after being unable to be with one another in that way for so long. Our continuing every night since and squirm at the idea of tonight being no different. As I submerge deeper into what will be tonight my cell begins to ring. Who would be calling me at this time and on my cell? I climb out of my long awaited bath and answer my phone which is on my dresser.*

Hello?

Beth... Beth sorry to call you so late.

Hi Charles. No problem - let me get Kevin for you.

His voice rising a bit No Beth I called to speak to you.

Charles you're scaring me. Is everything okay *alarmed* Is JD. Alright?

Beth....... Blanche passed away earlier today

Oh.... Is JD. Okay?

He didn't want me to call anyone

You mean he didn't want you to call Kevin?

Beth..... He needs

Interrupting Charles set up our travel for the morning. Kevin and I will be ready.

Beth..... Beth I don't think, Kevin will not be so willing

Regardless of his relationship with Blanche he adores and cares greatly for his grandfather. I will take care of Kevin. And please do not say anything to JD, he will probably try to talk us out of coming,

Beth,..... Thank you.

I hang up with Charles and sit on the edge of the bed. I gather my thoughts and gather my words. I prepare myself for the debate that will most likely take place. After a few minutes I swallow deeply and head down to the study. I tap lightly on the door and the response "come in" *is heard instantly.*

Entering I find Kevin sitting on the leather black sofa that houses several important looking documents. His laptop on his side and a pad and pen in his hand. In the background the sound of Ray Charles playing. But not the crisp sound from a CD but rather the actual album playing with scratches and all.

You do know compact disc is the latest trend.

Pulling me onto his lap, I know I heard the racket you were making upstairs. I peeked in and heard you listening to Ray. That's what prompted me to turn him on down here.

You could have said hello

Oh no I could not. If I had, no work would get done *kissing me on my neck.*

Hey hey none of that. I came down to talk to you. *Rubbing his nose into my neck* Everything okay?

....

Reacting to my silence Kevin stops and looks into my eyes. Beth are you okay? Mandy?

I just hung up with Charles. JD is ok but Blanche passed away earlier today. *Presenting stunned for a brief second Kevin returns to kissing my neck and making his way to my chest.* Kevin... Kevin look at me. Charles is arranging our travel. We will leave in the morning.

Continuing his invasion on my chest Beth "we" aren't going anywhere.

Kevin, we are! *Sensing his anger building, I stand then kneel to his side.* Kevin, the man I love with all I have, this is something we must do. Not for Blanche but for JD.

Beth you don't understand

And I may never understand but Blanche was a part of JD's world for over fifty years, his wife. Imagine you losing me.

Shaking his head I brought him back to when he almost did.

Baby JD needs you right now. Other than Blanche you are all he has.

Tears forming in Kevin's eyes, sighing We will go.

If it is alright with you I would like to ask Mrs. Clarke to come along and ask if we can stay at her home.

In a low tone, I will set things up with Mrs. Clarke. *Hugging me tightly* Thank you!

Kissing his lips I love you.

And I love you. *Standing now* I'm going to talk with Mrs. Clarke. When I'm done I would love to have you in my arms, close to me.

Kissing Kevin once again no other place I would rather be.

****

We land in Houston early afternoon. The mood so far has been light. Kevin at times presenting pre-occupied but Amanda's demand for her dad's attention brings him back to us. Arriving first to Mrs. Clarke's home we settle in for a bit, leaving Amanda in Mrs. Clarke's care. Donaldson and Thomas left behind to keep watch. Kevin and I head to JD's with Erickson traveling in the car directly behind us.

During the drive I take Kevin's hand into mine and squeeze gently. I see the uneasiness in his eyes. Pulling through the privacy gate he tenses even more and my heart sinks. I recall his last visit here as a child and the horrific words he heard about himself and his mother. I swallow hard, swallowing the cry that was starting. Once through the gate Charles meets us as we pull in front of the house. Erickson in the car behind us, drives pass the front to the back. Kevin presenting hesitant to exit the car sits for a moment. Not releasing his hand I turn to him.

I know how hard this is for you. For once lean on me. I'm not fragile and stronger than you think.

Sighing, thank you *kissing my hand.* Knowing you are here with me helps more than you will ever know.

Stepping out the car Kevin is greeted by Charles. The two shake and a non- verbal exchange that only Charles and Kevin understands. Kevin then makes his way to my side of the car and opens the door for me.

After hugging Charles, we are led into the house, to
JD's Study.

Tap... Tap

Not now.

Opening the door Then when?

Voice cracking Beth, Beth what are you doing
here?

Not answering and stepping aside to allow Kevin's
entrance. No words exchange initially when JD see's
Kevin. Rather the two embrace and hold each other
for what seems like an eternity, emotions overcome
them both. My own waterworks begin.

Pulling themselves apart JD wipes his eyes You
kids shouldn't have made this trip

Yes we did *hugging JD myself now.*

His voice quivering did my great- granddaughter
too make the trip?

She did. Both she and Mrs. Clarke are back at the
house.

Sighing She would love it here. *As quickly as the*
words come out his mouth is as quickly as he realizes
what was said.

Maybe next time grandfather. How are you doing?

I'm doing just fine. Did Simon Send you the specs?

As the two avoid the reason for our travel to Texas I begin to explore JD's office. Before this moment JD didn't fit the stereotypic Texan but seeing the place he does his business, "everything is bigger in Texas" fits. A large mahogany desk placed in what he calls his home office. Wall to wall bookcases filled to capacity, a large leather sofa with an equally large round table fills the room. On the walls elk, deer and I think a bison head? On his desk and the table behind his desk pictures on top of pictures. But what catches my eye are the two pictures housed in the center of his desk. A very young JD with his beautiful bride. The two look impeccable and in love. I smile at the site of the younger JD. The other eye catcher, a beautiful silver frame with Amanda's picture. Across the bottom reads "Grandpa's Girl". I question eternally if Blanche acknowledged the picture or better yet acknowledged she had a granddaughter. As I continue my scouting, a young black woman enters with coffee and tea.

Thank you Tessa. Please make sure Sarah knows it will be three of us for supper.

Kevin immediately responding No grandfather, I don't want to....

Interrupting Thank you JD Kevin and I - We would love to stay for dinner *avoiding any contact with Kevin*

Wonderful. You know you kids are welcome to stay here.

Kevin insuring I make no such commitment By now Mrs. Clarke probably has Mandy settled in.

JD can we help with any of the arrangements?

No... *Smiling* Blanche was a woman who knew what she liked and wanted.

Taking JD's hand Are you okay?

Beth I am. *Changing the subject back to the acquisition he and Kevin were discussing.*

Taking the hint Excuse me JD while you and Kevin talk do you mind if I see if I could be of some assistance in the kitchen?

Beth you don't need permission to walk the hallways of this house. Please move about freely.

Then I leave you two to whatever you two are working on. *I exit JD's office without foolishly asking to be directed to the kitchen. Roaming the halls per say, I take note of the southern plantation style home, beautifully decorated with not even a hair out of place. Entering the formal dining room the sentiment of everything is bigger in Texas once again an understatement but certainly befitting here. The thick mahogany wood table must seat at least ten comfortably. The chandelier hanging above looks as if it was taken straight from the movie set of Gone With The Wind. Absolutely breathtaking! If I don't learn anything more about Blanche I can definitely say she had impeccable taste.*

Finally ending in the kitchen I find an older black women and Tessa busy at work preparing supper.

Hello I'm Elizabeth, Kevin's wife

Mrs. Walker a pleasure to meet you, I'm Ms. Sarah can I get you something?

I thought I could help with dinner?

The two women exchanging eye contact.

Thank you, but no we have it.

Would you mind if I made myself a cup of tea?

Mrs. Walker I could make you a cup of tea. Where would you like me to serve it?

Tessa is it?

Yes

Tessa no trouble to do it myself *and before giving her an opportunity to prevent me from doing so I take the kettle from the stove and add water. Then place on the burner.*

Would you like a piece of sweet potato pie with that?

Thank you Ms. Sarah but the tea is all.

Did Anna-Mae Come in with you?

Who?

Anna-Mae Clarke?

I should be ashamed that I don't know Mrs. Clarke's first name. Yes she did. She is at her home caring for my daughter. You know Mrs. Clarke?

Certainly. Anna-Mae and I have known each other since grade school. We speak at least once a week.

Oh

Yes lord we speak often. Mostly me trying to get her back home at least for a visit but she says her family is in New York.

Her family, if Kevin had heard this he would not blink an eye. He sees her just the same, his family.

And that baby of yours, she sounds like a little gem.

Smiling, she is. You've met Kevin?

Many times. He and my youngest son played summer sports together when Kevin would visit for the summer.

Here you are... *And as Kevin confirms finding me he takes sight of Ms. Sarah and hugs her tightly.*

My baby boy. Look how big and handsome you are.

And you're as beautiful as ever.

Smiling from ear to ear, you know that's right. How are you baby?

You met my wife, since Beth and now our daughter life couldn't better.

When will I get to meet that beautiful baby?

How soon can you visit Mrs. Clarke? I know she is looking forward to seeing you.

This evening, as soon as I get off. How long will you be in town?

Just a few days.

Well I'm so glad you came *hugging Kevin once more.* I know this trip is difficult for you but I am very proud of you for coming. Yes – yes, bless your heart baby because I know firsthand how that woman treated you. Yes lord bless your heart.

Instantly Kevin begins to tense. The discussion putting attention on Blanche and Kevin's past re-establishes the uneasiness – uncomfortableness Kevin was feeling on the drive over. I see it in his face and body movement. Interrupting So you and JD are all done discussing business?

Trying to pull himself from his past I repeat the question twice before Kevin responds

Yes... Ahh Ms. Sarah Would it be possible to pack up what you prepared for dinner?

Kevin sure honey but why?

Confused by his request as well Kevin?

It would do grandfather some good to get out of the house. I will call Mrs. Clarke and let her know we are on our way.

Realizing he reached his limit here I dare not challenge his decision but agree. That's a great idea. You talk to JD and I'll call Mrs. Clarke.

Taking my hand in his Kevin squeezes gently then kisses me on the cheek.

Within thirty minutes and no argument from JD myself, Kevin and JD arrive to Mrs. Clarke's home. Entering the house to our surprise Adele and John greet us. Adele sensing the tension in her grandson takes him into her arms and hold on for an extended embrace. She then turns to JD.

So sorry for your loss.

Hugging Adele Thank you *quickly changing the subject* Where is my Amanda Rose?

Mrs. Clarke enters the kitchen with my sweet baby girl in her arms. Before she has a chance to hand Amanda to me JD immediately upon seeing her takes Amanda from Mrs. Clarke and without any words exchanged exits the kitchen. Everyone internally understands his need, makes no move to follow or ask where he was going. Instead the women begin setting up for dinner and Kevin, John, Charles and Erickson head out to the back patio.

Beth baby how's my grandson?

Adele he's dealing as best as he can. Flying out for JD was the easy part. Physically being in Blanche's home presented to be a bit challenging.

Is he planning on attending services?

Sighing Truthfully Adele seeing how uneasy - uncomfortable Kevin was today if he chooses not to go I will support him completely and I will go and support JD.

Baby I was Surprise he came out.

He loves JD.

I know he does. That's why John and I flew out. Anything we can do to help and support not just my grandson but you as well, my granddaughter we are here.

Hugging Adele Thank you. *Releasing from our embrace I wipe away the tears that managed to escape. Tears resulting from her attentiveness.* I'm going to check on JD and Amanda.

Entering the living room I find Amanda sleep in her great-grandfather's arms. JD startled by my entrance immediately wipes away the tears streaming down his face. I hug JD and kiss him on his forehead. JD let me take her.

No no no she is fine right where she is at.

JD can I get you anything?

Inhaling deeply Beth no fussing over me. I'm okay. Really.

You just lost your wife, the love of your life. I will not accept being ok!

Forcing a smile Beth....

Taking his right hand into mine Over the past year you have filled a void that only a father can fill. No greater father to me then mine but you come darn close. With all my baggage you have welcomed me with no questions. You sat with me day after day, don't think I didn't notice. *Smiling* You remembered me telling you about the one book I never had time to finish, "The Good Earth" by Pearl Buck. Day after day while I laid in that hospital bed you read to me. From beginning to end.

With tears in his eyes You heard me?

I did and by my bedside is where I keep my 1st Edition, not to read but as a reminder of you when I wake in the morning and when I go to bed in the evening.

Emotion presented by his quivering voice Beth *squeezing my hand.*

Now it is time to lean on me. You and I, we have an unspeakable bond. You and I have something that no others would ever understand.

I love you Beth.

And I hope you know I love you.

I do and from the first day I met you I understood why my grandson fell in love with you. You have been a God send to both of us.

I'm going to tell you what I keep telling your grandson, you two are my miracles.

Beth *sighing deeply* Blanche was diagnosed with Alzheimer's disease about five years ago.

Oh JD I'm sorry.

Over the past year she began to really decline hence the hospital episode.

JD why didn't you say something?

Nothing to be said, Blanche was a proud women.

JD I'm sorry.

Don't be. Blanche and I had our troubles but she was my first love. That woman and I weathered the unimaginable, burying our son. But we got through it together. I find comfort knowing my son and Blanche are together after being apart for so long. *Stifling his emotion* I have my memories and thanks to you, Kevin and this beautiful joy here in my arms I look forward to tomorrow.

Oh JD.

And once change in power takes place I plan on spreading my time with this little one. I have an opportunity I thought I would never have and I plan on enjoying every day I have left with her.

Hugging JD I can't wait. Come on now, let's join the others.

Chapter 08: Beyond Death

Kevin and I arrive to JD's home exactly at 8:30 a.m. Different then yesterday, the quiet - mellow atmosphere has significantly changed. Entering the foyer Ms. Sarah greets both Kevin and I, extending her embrace and whispering "Her family came in early this morning. Baby talk to your granddaddy, he's in his office".

Kevin immediately presenting concerned takes my hand and we make our way through the noticeable crowd to JD's office. As we pass a forced courteous smile presents itself from the many faces followed by whispers. Kevin too noticing, takes me by the waist to move me along a bit faster ending at JD's door. Knocking once and not waiting for a response, Kevin enters with me by his side. JD at his desk with stacks of papers in front of him.

Grandfather is everything okay?

Just going over the acquisition proposal Simon sent over yesterday evening.

Grandfather we can go over the terms later today. Right now we should be heading to the church.

JD no longer able to sustain himself throws his hands to his face and releases into them. Immediately to his grandfather's side Kevin takes JD into his hold. Seeing two men I find the strongest examples of men falling apart right in front of me brings on my own water works. Not sure what to say or do I stand frozen in place until the release from one another.

Baby could I have a moment alone with grandfather?

Relieved by the request for my absence I reply immediately Sure. *Walking to the door with my back to them I continue* I'm blessed to have had three men in my life who I adore. One is in heaven and the other two are in this room. I love both of you dearly. *Continuing not to look either of them in the face for my own selfish reason of not wanting to breakdown completely I exit JD's office closing the door behind me. I decide to make my way to the kitchen in hopes of finding Ms. Sarah, the only other person I know and would feel somewhat comfortable with this very moment. On my way I hear a low southern female voice calling after me.*

Elizabeth...... Elizabeth!

Turning to the voice I'm confronted by an older white women who resembles an older Blanche Yes?

Honey I thought I would have to sprint to catch up with you. *Extending her hand* I'm Savannah Blanche's sister.

Ms. Savannah a pleasure to meet you.

Do you have a moment?

Wanting desperately to say no yes flows so easily.

Let's talk in the parlour.

Following Ms. Savannah I become a bit concerned with what the topic will be.

Have a seat. I hear my sister had a great-granddaughter.

Yes ma'am.

Is she here?

No Ma'am.

Is she here in town?

Yes Ma'am. She's being cared for by Mrs. Clarke.

How is Anna Mae?

Well *I assume* well

You give her my regards. Well you're probably wondering why this old women wants to talk to you.

Smiling I am curious.

I would like to talk to you about my sister

Feeling uneasy If this has anything to do with my husband well frankly I think Kevin should be a part of any conversation better yet spoke with directly, not me.

Blanche said you were no nonsense and blunt.

Please I do not mean any disrespect.

And none presumed. *Pulling an envelope from her pocketbook* Blanche wanted me to give you this?

Presenting both puzzled and extremely uncomfortable Me?

Yes you. I ask that you wait a bit to read it and read it alone initially.

Shit I can only assume by the recommendation this letter will only piss Kevin off.

I'm not sure I should

Cutting me off in midsentence You don't owe my sister anything however I ask that you oblige her last and only request.

Without verbally responding I accept the envelope in hand.

Good. I guess we should get going *halting in place* and although I've threatened each and every family member please ignore any and all asinine questions and comments.

Questions? Comments?

Dear girl your husband was and is an urban legend. *Laughing* probably wrong choice of words but they knew he existed but Blanche had a way of controlling situations and this, her grandson one of them.

And the reason, his race!

Unfortunately Yes. I will be 81 years young next week and in all my 81 years the south is what it was and for my family mixing races was unheard of, not allowed. *Expressing a concerned look* With all that boy heard - what he was taught. In a million years I would never expected him to fall in love with a black girl. Never!

Curiosity getting the best of me Did you approve?

I can't say that I did. But different from my sister I traveled the world, living in France for many years. When lynching and beatings were happening in Mississippi I was in Europe where interracial relationships were more acceptable, where blacks were more respected. My disapproval came from a place of concern. What my nephew would endure, how Kevin's mother would be treated. Society, the south was not ready for such a relationship regardless how evolved people say we are. See my family built my hometown. Employed many and kept the economy going for over a hundred years. We had the largest Tobacco and Cotton plantations in the south. My father and grandfather were fair men, employing anyone who needed work. But that was as far as it could go. Then my sister marrying JD, the love of her life. What my Nephew was going to represent, being in the public eye, an interracial relationship was not appropriate. But if I could take it all back, encourage his happiness and supporting the fight - so much would be different. So much!

Did Blanche regret any...

Interrupting my sister regretted it all. She blamed only herself and when she finally overcame her fears of confronting the situation well she was called home. *Standing* We better get going my sister detested delays and tardiness.

Standing as well I extend me hand Thank you for giving me some sort of clarity.

My dear the door is open now, you and my great nephew are family. Whatever time I have left and as long as I have my scruples the door is open.

Hugging Ms. Savannah Thank you.

****

Services for Blanche was actually quite beautiful. A packed church with family and friends from almost everywhere. More surprising, the many blacks that came to pay their last respects and showing genuine emotions.

JD maintained as long as he could, well he lasted as long as one would expect. It wasn't until the end when final respects were offered - prior to her casket being closed and with everyone out of the church JD had his last moment with Blanche. Refusing to leave his grandfather during this time I stood in the back of the church while JD and his only grandson stood side by side, looking down upon Blanche. Kevin consoling his grandfather but I know in his heart he too is mourning not only Blanche but all that have gone before her. Finally in some sense coming to terms with his mother and father's deaths.

Her obituary mentioning not only Kevin's mom but him, me and our pride and joy. And in that moment of it being read to the congregation I felt the nervous shake coming from Kevin. Taking my hand into his as though he was consoling me. On the other side JD too taking my hand and grasping firmly.

Returning to JD's home after the burial, crowds poured in and out until about five in the evening. Once only JD's closest friends and Savannah was left stories of Blanche were shared. JD reviewing his first encounter with Blanche and how at first sight falling in love. He talked about the birth of their son being their happiest day then referring to the darkest, when Kevin's father was killed. Holding his own, on the surface JD is getting through it. But eternally I know he's only getting through this because of his grandson.

Because I know the Joy Amanda brings her grandfather and with Kevin's permission I asked JD to take a walk with me, asking him to show me his beautiful property. Agreeing immediately we walk out the back where JD is met by Mrs. Clarke and Amanda. Mrs. Clarke and JD extending an embrace I excuse myself with Amanda. Returning inside I introduce my baby-girl to her great- great aunt Savannah.

Beth what a beautiful gem.

Thank you.

I see why JD couldn't do anything but rave about her.

Smiling Yes she definitely has an effect on JD.

Well she is certainly precious.

Do you have any children?

No, I was never planted in one place long enough. I was wife and mother to my career.

What did you do?

Fashion photographer. One of the few female fashion photographers back then.

Wow *realizing the reason she lived in Europe.* How long did you live overseas?

Left when I was 20 and came back to the states, New York initially at the age of 62. I moved back to Mississippi just a few years ago.

Immersed in Savannah's life I don't realize Kevin's absence until he returns with JD and Mrs. Clarke.

Savannah let me have my great-granddaughter.

JD you were correct, she is absolutely beautiful. Anna Mae, how are you darling?

Kissing Mrs. Savannah Doing wonderful and you look great.

Interrupting the conversations taking place Grandfather Beth and I are going to head over to Mrs. Clarke's.

Before you two go, could I ask you to take a drive with me?

Grandfather it is getting late and

Interrupting it will only take a few minutes

Turning to me Beth?

You know I could never say no to you JD, so come on you two.

Taking my hand into his And I'm going to hold you to that.

With JD leading, the three of us climb into the chauffeured Mercedes. Charles and JD's driver in the front with JD myself and Kevin in the backseat. Driving in the car behind us, Erickson. After about a ten minute drive we pull onto a winding road that is at least two miles long. Driving on this road reminds me of my last visit to the Queens Botanical Garden. Beautiful seasonal trees lined the property and although winter, the mild heat - southern weather allows for seasonal blooming flowers, green grass and leaves on trees. A far distance from a NY winter.

I know you kids are planning on leaving in the morning but I was hoping maybe you would stay until after the gala.

Grandfather we need to head back. Besides *laughing* sleeping in a twin size bed with a women who needs a California king is far from comfortable.

Funny Mr. Walker really funny

We are here

Grandfather?

Taking a ring of keys from his suit jacket Your wedding present *and the keys are placed into my hands.*

JD absolutely not. You already gave us a gift!

Young lady just a few minutes ago you told me you couldn't say no to me.

Grandfather Beth is correct, we can't accept.

You can and you will. *Motioning for Kevin and I to get out of the car.* I will be at Mrs. Clarke's for the evening spending time with my Amanda Rose. Everything you two need is here.

Kevin?

Don't look at me. I had no idea, none-whatsoever.

With his last words lingering, JD pulls off. I assume Erickson coming along was part of his plan, to insure we had a way back to Mrs. Clarke's.

Are you familiar with the area?

Smirking Yes, but I'll let you take all this in first to form your own opinion.

Flashing my disapproval look. Just about to open the front door, it opens with a middle aged business attired black woman on the other side Hello Mr. and Mrs. Walker, welcome to your new home. I'm Donna Jefferies and I work for Durand Holdings. I've been assigned to assist you Mrs. Walker as your assistant.

Stepping into the grand foyer I Look to Kevin An assistant?

Shrugging his shoulders Not a bad idea!

I assisted Mr. Durand with the purchase. Can I give you two a tour?

Kevin answering immediately "Yes" *because he senses my "this is absolutely ridiculous" comment coming forth. Taking my hand in his we tour the over ten thousand square foot home offering seven bedrooms, nine bathrooms, a catering kitchen and a family kitchen, butler's quarters, a study, two home offices and sauna. The immediate backyard a home owners dream, resembling the Botanical Garden scene seen when driving up to the house.*

We will head over to the stables now.

Stables? JD better not have *and just as expected two beautiful horses are in the arenas just outside the stable* Kevin?

Once again shrugging his shoulders

Kevin we need to talk to JD immediately. We can't accept any of this and horses, we won't be here often nor long enough to care for them. *Then it dawned on me* We can't afford horses!

Beth take a breath, it is fine?

Getting pissed How so?

Squeezing my hand gently I take Kevin's hint of not debating the issue with Donna directly in our presence.

Mrs. Walker if I can answer a few of your questions. The horses are and will be cared for. Past the east meadow, few miles up is where a few of the farm hands reside. They take care of the property as well as the horses. You also have a trainer that comes by daily to work both.

Training?

Both are top champion breeds.

I continue to express my disapproval by shaking my head

It seems that I have overwhelmed you enough *smiling* if you require any further assistance *handing me her card* please do not hesitate to call. I will be back tomorrow at 9?

No we will be flying home tomorrow.

Oh *presenting surprised* I was under the impression that you and Mr. Walker would be staying until after the gala.

Kevin interrupting immediately We will call you later this evening and let you know our plans. *Extending his hand* Thank you for all that you have done. You and grandfather did an incredible job. The house, furnishings everything is perfect.

Thank you Mr. Walker.

Please call me Kevin. We will talk later.

I look forward to it. Good night then Mrs. Walker - Kevin.

Good night.

Kevin taking my hand once again, leads us back inside the massive house, leading us to the master suite. Kevin what are you doing?

Thought we would check out the bedroom again.

Kevin stop playing we need to talk about this. I need to get back to NY.

Beth why the rush?

Because I want to go home. We spent over a week in Lake Tahoe and wasn't home for a hot minute before receiving the call about Blanche.

You still haven't given me a reason why we need to rush back

Because my sister.

Cynthia? If your concern is for Cynthia we will fly her out.

Really…. One cockyass answer Mr. Walker.

Come on you know I did not mean it that way. I'm just reminding you that we have the resources to have your sister come out for as long as she wants.

Rolling my eyes Whatever Kevin

Grasping me by my waist Baby I have too much that needs to be completed by the end of the month, before JD steps down.

I understand that part. I just don't get why it can't be done from NY?

I need to work here in Houston, from the home office.

My anger building by every word coming out of Kevin's mouth You had this planned?

Beth how? You talked me into flying out here.

117

Realizing he is correct I soften my look Yes I did. Kevin this is just so overwhelming.

Beth I had no idea grandfather was going to do this but the timing is perfect. If you don't like any of it, the furnishings, staff, anything we will change it immediately.

When you say staff you are referring to the farm guys right?

Laughing No Beth. I'm referring to the housekeepers, cook etc.

Don't freaking sugar coat this Mr. Walker. You mean a maid, chef

Well yes

Shaking my head. So we will fly back home immediately following the gala?

Yes.

Alright Mr. Walker but where do we stay tonight?

Home!

Home huh... We are home. Well let's get our baby girl then.

But first *unbuttoning my blouse*

Really?

With a teasing expression Oh really!

You know I could never say no to you

That's what I'm banking on Mrs. Walker, That's what I'm banking on *and I'm kissed passionately.*

Chapter 09: Change In Power

Sitting here at my kitchen table I put together the final touches for today's events. I rush through my list to insure all is done so I will be able to give my full attention to our family. Cynthia and Kevin's grandparents flew in late last night after being delayed by a snowstorm on the east coast. With our immediate family here the feeling of completion sets in, I am ready for what this busy extraordinary day has in stored. However the real event takes place at noon today when JD officially steps down as CEO and President of Durand Holdings and hands the reins over to his grandson, my husband - CEO and President of one of the wealthiest companies in the world. Wow just think when I first met Kevin I took him for an absolute pain in the ass. Stalker even. I smile at the thought of my man, so proud of what he accomplished and what he has overcome. More importantly my heart is full knowing he and his grandfather has a relationship - bond that no one can break. The bridge finally complete. But enough of this, six in the morning and I need to prepare for the caterer's arrival. As JD requested I'm going big from the start of the day to the end. The day will begin with breakfast for the immediate family, being served promptly at 7. Kevin and JD will head into the office like any other day but promptly at noon with the complete board, family, close friends and other business partners - associates change in power will occur. As I continue to run through my day I hear a voice that puts an instant smile on my face.

I rolled over to hopefully continue from last night and you were gone.

A lot to do today and wanted to get an early start.

Pulling me to my feet and into his embrace Good morning Mrs. Walker

Smiling ever so large Good Morning Mr. Walker can I fix you a cup of coffee?

No I have something else in mind *taking my hand into his Kevin leads us to his office. Once in the door is closed and locked and my disrobing begins*

Kevin we can't, not now

Oh yes we can *and as Kevin continues his attempt to undress me we hear the cry of our baby girl over the monitor.*

Just when I was giving in.

Oh but baby we will pick this up again tonight. Do I have your word you will continue this evening?

Do you really need to ask? *Shaking my head* You relax and I will take care of Amanda. You have a full day ahead of you.

Beth I really want you to think about a Nanny especially if you're not going to let Mrs. Clarke help us.

Kevin I'm not comfortable with strangers taking care of Amanda right now and as to Mrs. Clarke I wanted her to enjoy herself while we are here, not to feel obligated.

She doesn't Beth

We will revisit this tomorrow. For now I suggest you get a few more minutes of peace because the craziness is about to begin.

Making my way upstairs I find Amanda no longer crying but staring up and laughing. Like I always do when I see her in this way I recite "Good Morning baby girl who is watching over you today? Is it Grandpa Frank? Grandma Amanda or Grandpa Jackson? I know it is Rosie and Rosa? But wait you have one more angel looking over you, is it Great-grandma Blanche"? *With each person announced the smile and cooing - giggles even continue. Picking Amada up into my arms I whisper in her ear* "whomever is here you tell them mommy and daddy loves and misses them all okay"? *Her response a big ole smile. Just then Kevin enters*

Hi Mandy you want to hang with dad?

Kevin you have a big day ahead of you, I have our daughter.

Regardless of how big or small my day is you and Amanda will always come first.

Kevin that was a promise you made me some months ago, I don't hold you to it anymore. I've seen how hard you have worked these past few weeks trying to do everything here from the house and limiting your traveling. Seeing all that you do I know it is impossible to continue doing so.

You two will always be my first priority. Yes very shortly I will need to travel but I'm hoping you two will be traveling with me.

We will have this discussion later sir. *Just then the doorbell rings* You get yourself ready Amanda and I will get the caterers setup.

Shaking his head to show his disapproval You do know you have two maids!

We have two housekeepers and one of which I gave the next few days off.

Why Beth?

Because I'm here, Adele, Cynthia and Mrs. Clarke are here. We are all women that can do for ourselves and do not like being fussed over.

Waving his hands in the air as if surrendering Okay Mrs. Walker, you're the queen of our castles.

I thought I heard Amanda

Cynthia if only I met you first *kissing Cynthia on the cheek*

Trying her best not to blush I told you once before I'm too much woman for you *laughing* Good Morning.

Well if you two are done.

Girl *shaking her head at me* what can I help with?

Ladies I'm going to leave you two for now

Interrupting You mean three ladies because *taking Amanda from his arms* you need to get yourself ready.

Whispering but loud enough for Cynthia to hear You know what that authoritative tone does to me.

Blushing Get ready Mr. Walker, just get ready.

With Amanda in my arms Cynthia and I go down to the kitchen. I begin pacing a bit, trying to figure out what needs to be done next.

Hey stop for a minute, sit here.

Cynthia so much needs to get done

And it will. *Cynthia places a cup of fresh tea in front of me* Since the holidays I can count the number of conversations we have had

I know.

How are you?

I'm good, what about you?

No missy.... Are you sleeping?

I think it's the southern air, but yes I am.

Nightmares?

Over the past few weeks, very few.

Eating?

Cynthia....

Beth!

I am, I even put on a few pounds

Living in Texas works for you

Who knew me in the south and not having anything negative to say about it? But regardless I can't wait to go home.

You are home.

No NY is home for me you and Amanda.

Laughing And your husband?

Oh you know what I mean. Home will always be New York.

Home should be wherever your husband and child are at. Beth Texas could be home.

Hell no....NY is home with you and my nephews.

We will always be here for you. Don't feel obligated to return because if us.

Cynthia.....

Excuse me Mrs. Walker the caterers finished setting up.

Thank you Paula. I better check on Kevin. Cynthia can you take Amanda for a few minutes?

Do you even need to ask?

Hey baby girl go to Aunt Cynthia *placing Amanda into Cynthia's arms.*

Beth could I borrow one of your handbags?

Sure which one?

Anyone to go with my black dress.

Black dress?

Yes why?

No reason, just when you go up check the closet.

What?

Now you're hard of hearing? *I begin to laugh* just check the closet when you go back up.

Making my way upstairs I here Kevin in the shower. I restrain myself from joining him. Instead I make the bed then begin pulling handbags out from the closet. I identify a cute tote that will not only hold my things but a few of Amanda's necessities. I then eye my black coach that would go well with Cynthia's outfit. Opening the handbag I pullout items left in from my last use which by the contents was Blanche's funeral. Sifting through what to keep and what is trash, I find the envelope given to me by Ms. Savannah the day of the funeral. With all that has been going on I completely forgot about it. Do I read it now? My question answered by Kevin grasping me by my waist.

Why didn't you join me?

Because you have no time. The hanky panky can wait. Besides didn't you get enough last night?

Did you?

Trying to suppress my smile No I certainly did not.

And neither did I. But I will wait. What are you doing *releasing me from his hold*

Cynthia wanted to borrow a handbag.

I think you and Cynthia should do some shopping, my treat.

Really Kevin *presented in my usual displeased tone whenever the subject of shopping – spending money comes up*! Besides did I not go out yesterday and shop?

Yes you did and I've come to a conclusion?

What conclusion?

You will spend on everyone but yourself.

Get dressed Mr. Walker I'm going to check on Cynthia and Amanda *stuffing the envelope into my robe. Heading downstairs I hear Cynthia in her room.*

Hey

Everything is set downstairs. Adel and John just went down.

Let me guess Adele now has Amanda?

You guessed correctly.

I better head down

Beth *her voice cracking* the suit it is absolutely beautiful but I can't accept.

You can't accept?

I'm wearing my dress.

No you are not. *Taking a seat next to her on the chaise* Do you remember my Senior Prom?

Beth...

You made sure I had not only the most beautiful gown but had me go to Benny's salon for a full day treatment... From head to toe. Single mother of two, struggling - paid for everything because... Well I won't get on the mother wagon today but Cynthia if I didn't know then the hardship looking back I know what you sacrificed. Don't tell me you can't wear a suit that for years you had your eye on. And no offense, my graduation you came damn close with the wannabe channel suit you wore. Now you have your Channel suit with Pravda shoes. Way overdue but you are going to accept it, wear it and not say another word.

You didn't buy me shoes!

Oh I did. So *standing* get up and get ready.

You know I love you Beth.

Every day of my life. *Hugging me the tears begin.*

Releasing me Go and get ready I will dress Amanda.

Cynthia I

Interrupting me Just do it and Thank you.

I should be thanking you but you're welcome.

Returning to my room I find Kevin completely dressed looking ever so fine as he always does in a suit. You looking very dapper Mr. Walker.

Flashing that devilish smile I can easily take it off

I would rather you take me with it on.

With a shocked look Really?

Laughing hard yes really but we will save it for tonight.

Tease.

Well everyone is gathering downstairs and JD should be here soon.

Then I still have a few minutes with you alone.

Yes you do. It gives me time to give you this *pulling a small box from my dresser drawer* Read the card later.

Doing just the opposite Kevin reads the card, tears develops in his eyes. Thank you baby. *Hugging me* I love you so much.

And I you, now open the box. I spent a little of your money.

Baby it is beautiful. What would make it even better is if you purchased as a pair, one for you.

I'm not a Rolex type of girl. Here, one more. *Laughing* This one I was able to pay for myself.

Opening the box to find an engraved monogram pen Baby it is perfect. I will carry it with me always and only use it on special occasions.

Like today Mr. Walker. I'm glad you like it.

Just then Kevin's cell rings. Looking at the number Beth I need to take this, I'll be in my office.

No problem..... I love you

Kissing me hard and I love you *smacking my behind* now get dressed.

Pulling off my robe to get into the shower the letter I tucked away earlier falls to the floor. Should I do this now? I begin to read.

Chapter 10: The Gala – The Beginning

Good evening ladies and gentleman, welcome to Durand Holdings Annual Gala. My name is Elizabeth Walker and I'm married to that very handsome gentleman standing there on the side. I wanted to start this evening off by first acknowledging the woman who year after year for the past 20'years put this shindig together, with this year being no different. Truth be told, it wasn't until this morning I had an understanding - the meaning behind this Gala. But after receiving clarity from the creator of this event directly *looking over at JD* I now know the significance of it all and accept with honor the roll of coordinating next year's gala and beyond. *Applause from the crowd*

In honor of Blanche I ask you to dig deep this year, bid high on the items offered through the auction and if you don't win hopefully you will make a donation to one of the three Charities this Gala has funded for the past 20 years. *Smiling* And when you make that donation keep in mind Blanche is looking down from above. I hear she was a force not to reckon with so make sure your donation meets her approval. *Laughter from the crowd.* So please raise your glass to toast the memory of a woman that has given back in her own way. To Blanche Francine Durand, a woman who will be missed by all those that have benefitted from her hard work and dedication. She is and will be missed by family and friends. To Blanche.

Walking back to where JD is standing he takes my hand, kisses me lightly on the lips and whispers in my ear "You read the letter" *whispering back,* I wish I would have done sooner but yes I did. *After another kiss JD takes a few steps forward to address the many party goers. Kevin with a confused look walks to where I stand, takes my hand and whispers* "That was unexpected". *I reply immediately* I'll explain later.

My beautiful granddaughter everyone. *Turning back to me again* I love you darling. *I mouth* And I you. *Turning back to the crowd* Now y'all know I'm a man of a few words but after today's events I seem to be unable to keep this old mouth shut *chuckles and laughter from the crowd.* Today at noon I stepped down as CEO and President of Durand Holdings and turned the reins over to my grandson Kevin Walker *applause from the crowd.* Several years ago I knew there could be no other replacement but him to run a company I built from the ground up. I needed someone at the helm who shared my vision, value and views and when my grandson confirmed he would pick up where I'm leaving off I was overjoyed. But more importantly relieved. Then today's news confirmed what I already knew. Today my grandson proved he is more than a replacement but a trend setter - a visionary himself. Through his actions he silenced all the doubters.

A few years ago Kevin suggested we enter the technology world by purchasing a small company - Global Dynamics. A company so small with no more than 15 employees. Well if your head wasn't in the sand this past week you are aware of the History Durand Holdings made with selling Global Dynamics for a record amount of 2.1 billion dollars. Initiated, negotiated and completed all by my grandson Durand Holding new CEO and President, I have to say it again my grandson Kevin Jackson Walker. *Applause and whistling from the crowd.*

With my hand in his Kevin takes two steps forward. Thank you grandfather. Ladies and gentleman I learned all that I know about this business from this man *turning to JD*. Grandfather without your guidance and support *Kevin's voice begin to shiver - he pauses for a few seconds* this could not be. Losing my parents at an early age my grandparents stepped in and molded me into the man I am today. Adele, John and JD thank you. And by my side my beautiful wife and at home my baby girl *looking at me* excuse me our baby girl *laughing from the crowd.* I'm honored and truly humbled. Although I could never fill his shoes, I look forward to building onto the legacy my grandfather built. Now grandfather *turning to JD* I know you say your retired but I know I will have you by my side. I hope to make you proud *applause from the crowd.*

Son you already have. *Hugging Kevin.* But retirement, I'm a phone call away. If anyone is looking for me you will find me with my sweet great-granddaughter. She and I have big plans *ahh's and laughter.* Okay everyone If you don't have a glass please take one now. *Raising his glass* to my grandson, I'm proud of you. To Kevin Jackson Walker - Durand Holdings President and CFO. *Clinks and cheers fills the room.*

I would like to toast my grandfather as well, thank you for believing in me. Thank you for taking me under your wing. To Jackson Montgomery Durand a leader, visionary and one of the two greatest men in my life. I love you.

"Here Here" *from the crowd followed by cheers, applause and laughter.*

JD trying to restrain the emotions fighting to surface Okay enough of this, let's get this evening started. Maestro music please *and in a flash, the atmosphere transitions to an upbeat lively party* scene.

****

Come here....

Oh Mr. Walker bossiness kicking in?

Dance with me

The band begins Playing What A Difference A Day Made. Kevin begins singing

What a difference a day made

Twenty four little hours

Brought the sun and the moon

Where there use to be rain

His tipsy extra flirtatiousness melts me completely. Holding me firm against him while discretely caressing my lower back Kevin we aren't alone.

Don't care. This night is about us *and I'm pulled into him tighter.*

You're drunk

Flashing that gorgeous smile I am baby. Tonight I proved to myself I got this.

You should be proud I know JD is.

Are you proud of me?

Me?

You! *Caressing my behind*

Foolish question, I'm your loudest cheerleader.

Twirling me And I'm yours

But with all this *waving my arms* I will always be my father's child - that girl from Queens.

I wouldn't want it any other way.

You do know your parents are smiling down on you!

....

Both of them have always been proud of you.

....

Here I go And Blanche she too is proud

....

Kevin listen to me, Blanche was proud of her grandson and in her own way loved you.

Beth let's not do this

Just hear me out, you need to hear this.

Later

No now. You assume Blanche hated you, who you were - who you are but she didn't

What is all this about? Your introductions now this?

The day of Blanche's funeral, Savanah gave me a letter, a letter from Blanche.

Kevin stops in place, anger written all across his face

Take that look off you face Mr. Walker. The letter was her peace offering.

Why didn't you tell me about this?

Leading Kevin in another slow dance Because her request was for me to read it alone. I forget all about the letter until this morning, when I found it in one of my purses.

....

Kevin do you remember when we were in the Hamptons and JD told you he and Blanche wanted to purchase us a house, something in the city?

Kevin dismisses the question by shrugging his shoulders.

JD was sincere when he said your grandmother and I. Kevin Blanche wanted to do that for you.

....

Our home here, Blanche picked out the home.

....

Are you listening to me?

Beth I

Kevin the woman loved you. She didn't know how to tell you I assumed because she was ashamed for her past actions but she did. She spoke of our daughter as though she knew her. She experienced Amanda through JD's eyes.

I feel Kevin's body tense more

Kevin *stopping in place* she loved your daughter. *Smiling* "Every little girl deserves a pony. Special little girls deserves two". She wanted Amanda to have the horses.

She writes a letter instead of confronting me, words on a piece of paper.

Words of remorse, humbleness whatever we want to label it but the facts will be unchanged, she loved you.

Shaking his head She had an opportunity, at the hospital she could have

Interrupting Kevin the woman was suffering from Alzheimer's for years. In her own words, when she saw you she saw her son. For a quick second she had her son back.

Beth...

Face it, you my handsome husband was loved and is loved. Be proud of who you are, be proud of your accomplishments because everyone one in your life certainly is. *Caressing his cheek and looking directly into his eyes* Are you proud of all that you have accomplished?

I've come to value my possibilities.

But no longer possibilities Kevin. Baby you have succeeded and exceeded all expectations, even your own.

What I said earlier, if not for you I wouldn't be here right now.

I don't believe that. At some point you would have come to your senses and made the right choice.

Baby I doubt it. You however helped me see life in a whole different light. You give me life in ways you will never understand.

So Mr. CEO and President of Durand Holdings I think the band is playing our song now, ready to take my hand and lead me to love land?

Oh you know I am but first *pulling an envelope from the inside of his tuxedo jacket.* For you

What is it?

Open it..

Pulling out what looks like legal papers. I begin to read Deed to Said property located at.... Kevin what is this?

Property I acquired yesterday.

Property for what?

Property owned by you to do as you please. However I thought maybe you would like to open a center here in Houston.

Completely stunned Kevin I have the center in New York.

Yes you do. But I'm sure Texas could use the same support.

Kevin I don't know

Interrupting me No decision needs to be made right this minute, just think about it. But there's more in the envelope.

Looking further I find a check in the amount of five million dollars In a screechy voice Kevin?

I'm not the only one in power. As of this moment you are sole proprietor of your own foundation with a little money to start you off.

Speechless by his continued amazing generosity "little money"?

Yes

Kevin I can't."

Too late. Plus it sounds like a lot but realistically it isn't.

Blown completely away Thank you but how do you always manage to direct the attention away from yourself? This day, this night - this very moment is all for you.

No this day - my life is about you. Without you I wouldn't be here. This is our night baby, yours and mine.

Chapter 11: Some Truth

I lay still against Kevin's chest, feeling and hearing his accelerated heartbeat. This must be his third review of Blanche's letter. Giving away nothing, no remarks no sighs no expression at all. Unable to suppress my concern of how he is digesting the letter – the words she chosen I end the stifled silence Hey Mr. Walker are you okay

With a strained voice I am, just trying to wrap my head around all this.

A lot to take in but the end result *pulling myself up to be eye to eye with him* remains unchanged. At the end of the day you were, you are and is loved *kissing Kevin's lips.*

I still don't know how I feel but asking you to take over her charities, how do you feel about that?

When first reading the letter I was stunned but honored. Then Hearing from different people last night regarding how hard Blanche worked not just by raising money but actually making deliveries, served meals etc. I began to panic a bit. I'm not sure if I can even come close to what she did especially when our time here in Texas will be limited. I'm sure to do the job appropriately one would need to live here in a Texas fulltime.

Baby whatever you put your mind to you can do. Besides sounds like Blanche and you had similar work ethics.

I don't know Kevin. I'm just concerned with how much I could do from New York.

Well it seems she left you with not only her foundation but her most prized possession.

You read that too *smiling.*

She is correct, you do have a way with JD.

No JD just saw me as a possible connector for you and him.

Think that. I know my grandfather and he truly loves you.

I know he does and I love him as well. Not too many people take me in with all my baggage but JD did.

He loves you for you just as I do.

Oh Mr. Walker. *Yawning* Do you know it is going on 7 a.m.

Well I'm glad it is Saturday, we can spend the day right here *pulling me on top of him*

Mr. Walker not only are your grandparents here but my sister. Plus our daughter will be getting up soon.

Our family will be just fine. Mrs. Clarke invited everyone over for a day of fishing on the lake and by now everyone should have left.

Then we definitely need to get up *attempting once again to get up.*

Amanda is just fine. Between Gram, your sister and Mrs. Clarke she is better than fine.

Expressing my disapproval thorough my tone She went too?

Hush woman, it is you and me especially since I'll be flying out on Monday, which I hope to change your mind and have you and Amanda come with me.

Kevin I don't like the idea of being away from you either but I would rather use the time to see where to even start with the foundation and prepare for our return trip home. Besides you will be back on Wednesday and we all will be flying home on Thursday correct?

Yes ma'am.

Kevin

Baby by Thursday evening you will be in NY.
Now can we please get our workout on?

Pouting a bit Do you deserve a workout after
sending our family away with my daughter?

Laughing You do realize that I had something to
do with making your daughter which makes her our
daughter.

Don't try to change this around.

Hmmm, well I think I need to beg for forgiveness

*Starting at my midsection Kevin begins kissing
me, each time expressing his remorse ending at my
lips.*

Am I forgiven?

What else could I say Oh you are but I think I need
to experience how apologetic you are.

My pleading shall begin now.

****

*Saturday to this moment went by too fast. The
entire weekend I did all I could to not think about
Kevin's business meeting being held all the way
across the globe. When alone we loved each other
with extra emotions, when with our daughter we
reminded each other of our greatest achievement and*

when with our families we embraced how blessed we are. But my avoidance comes to an immediate halt. Time to face the dreaded moment.

Hey sweetheart what's wrong?

Tears falling This will be the first time we will be away from one another since *laughing with tears falling* that incident some time ago.

Kevin takes me into his arms, strokes my hair and whispers Come with me then. Just you me and Amanda.

Kevin I can't, you're flying to Nigeria of all places. I don't want to uproot Amanda on my insecurities and emotions.

Baby I can delay the meeting for a few days to allow you and Amanda time to prepare.

Mr. CEO and President of Durand Holdings what example would you be setting?

My family comes first and will always come first *kissing me on my lips.*

Kevin I'll be fine. Just promise you will stay in touch with me.

By the time you and Amanda are settled in for the evening I will be on the phone with both of you to talk, to listen, hell just to be close to you two. I've been dreading this trip since setting it up. Like you it hit me hard realizing we haven't been apart for almost two years.

Amanda and I will be fine knowing you will be thinking of us.

And I will, every second of the day.

Trying to stay strong You better get ready. *Attempting to climb out of bed I'm pulled back into Kevin's arms* Not so quick Mrs. Walker we need to go over a few rules.

Rules? Rules for who?

For you!

Expressed with pure New York attitude Excuse me?

Yes you heard me correctly.

Mr. Walker I don't know who you think you are talking to but

Interrupted I'm referring to you, Elizabeth! Because I'm not here doesn't mean rules are to be broken. Wherever you are security is to be with you. The same for Cynthia, my grandparents - everyone and especially you and my daughter. Am I making myself clear?

Whatever

Presenting with a stern look Beth I'm not joking!

I get it Kevin

Make sure you do. We talked about this already, you're not just that girl from Queens anymore. You're a very wealthy woman and with wealth all kinds come out. Please adhere to my request. I don't mean to scare you but the threats since my acceptance of this position *with a wary look* please do this.

Kevin I promise. Besides I'm sure Erickson will keep me in check.

Erickson flew back to New York Friday evening.

Concerned Is everything okay?

Yes he had some personal business to take care of.

Okay...

Charles will stay back.

Then who will be with you?

No worries I'm all taken care of.

Kevin

Ignoring my concern What are your plans?

I have enough to keep me busy which includes packing us up to go home.

Sighing You are home.

Hmmm New York is home, our primary home. Is that better?

Yes

Standing, Get ready Mr. Walker. I'm going down to get you a hot strong cup of coffee. When I return you should be showered and shaved.

With a salute Yes Ma'am. *We both laugh.*

Making my way down to the kitchen I find Cynthia already up doing the Sunday crossword from yesterday's paper.

Hey why are you up so early?

This is late for me. Besides I knew Kevin was leaving out this morning and wanted to see him off.

He'll be down soon. Can I fix you some breakfast?

No I'm good with the coffee *Cynthia confirms as she struggles with a pen.*

Laughing Do you need a pen Cynthia?

I guess I do.

I'll get you a few *laughing. I make my way to Kevin's office and just as I enter his cell rings.* Hello?

Good Morning can I speak to Mr. Walker?

I'm sorry Mr. Walker is not available at this time. This his wife how can I help you.

Mrs. Walker how are you?

I'm doing well, who am I speaking with?

Oh excuse me, my name is Caroline Davies, I'm one of the paralegals with Decker and Strickland. Mr. Strickland wanted to confirm that the fax was received?

I'll check, *walking over to the fax machine.* Yes I see something here. *And as I go through the pages my heart drops.*

Hello Mrs. Walker?

......

Mrs. Walker?

Umm sorry, yes the fax came through.

Please let Mr. Walker know the District Attorney is expecting a date by the end of today.

Date for what?

A date to meet with you. He was hoping to meet with you this week especially since the competency hearing is scheduled for Friday.

Huh.. Okay

Could you ask Mr. Walker to give Mr. Strickland a call back as soon as he can?

I will.

Great. Nice speaking with you Mrs. Walker

Same here, thank you and I hang up. I take a seat and begin to scan the 25 page document that details the last three months of my life. But what takes me completely off guard, a copy of the request to reject any bail. But bail for who? And there it is in black and white, NY State vs. Olivia Jenkins. Charging her with the murders of Rosa and Rosie and the kidnapping and attempted murder on Elizabeth Walker, me. What the fuck? In this moment I'm lost. Since being in Texas I was able to avoid thinking about the "incident" at the center, now I must. But how could this be? Angela confessed to everything. I heard it for myself. And all this time Kevin knew? Do I confront him and ask him why he has hidden all of this from me? Will he honest as to what is going on? As my thoughts retreat to the land of not trusting anyone I here Kevin's voice. I immediately stuff the packet behind the pillow on the coach and sit still just as Kevin enters.

Cynthia said you were in here.

She needed a pen and I sorta got distracted by a noticeable tear on the arm of the chair.

What tear? Looking intensely at the chair

Trying to produce a fake laugh Exactly! When I got closer it was just a hanging thread. Are you all ready?

Yes however I came down to steal you for a few more minutes.

Hmm. Well you found me.

Indeed I did. So you will be okay here?

Trying now to compress my anger I'm a big girl Mr. Walker. I do well fighting my own battles.

Never said you couldn't. *Looking a bit surprised by my comment.*

Softening my facial expression Sorry.... I will get better at this goodbye thing.

I hope this is the only goodbye you and I will be doing for a long time. *Pulling me into him* Next road trip I want both you and Amanda with me. Next time I will not take no for an answer.

Yes Mr. Walker *and I kiss Kevin passionately.* You better get going now you have a flight to catch.

It's our plane, not concern with it leaving without me.

Kevin....

Okay let me just kiss my baby girl again.

I'll get Amanda and meet you at the door.

Returning with Amanda in my arms Kevin is at the door as instructed. Seeing him ready to leave I begin to release my emotions although trying desperately to refrain from doing so. But as the waterworks begins everything I just learned in the past twenty minutes comes to the surface.

Stop it baby.

Trying to laugh I'm sorry...

Baby I can delay the meeting.

No, you need to go. I'll be fine.

You know I love you two *and Amanda and I are squeezed hard.*

And we love you. Now get out of here.

Kissing Amanda first Daddy is going to bring his baby girl back something very special. *Kissing me again* And you something extra special.

Smiling Get out of here.

I will call you as soon as we land.

Be *safe and the tears resume*

I will. We will be together in just a few short days okay?

I know we will.. I love you

And I love you too

I stand in the door and watch Kevin get into the awaiting car and pull off. Unable to stop the waterworks I return to his office to compose myself. But my mistake of returning where hard physical evidence lies, I begin to study the documents once again.

After a few minutes of dissecting the papers in my hand Cynthia comes in

Hey Beth everything okay?

Startled a bit by her entrance I am

What are you doing?

I thought I would look over some of the documents for the foundation *what a big freaking lie.* Just something to do to take my mind off of Kevin leaving.

Don't worry about Amanda *taking her from my arms* I thought I would take her to the park. You're welcome to join us.

Actually, you go on. A little work would do me some good. Donaldson and Thomas Will go along with you.

Both?

Absolutely *smiling* Mr. Walker wouldn't have it any other way. Besides I'll be here.

Okay then, maybe a movie later?

I'll even let you choose. Oops did I just say that?

Oh you certainly did. Alright I'll get Amanda ready. Don't worry about us, she and I will have a great day.

I'm not worried, in your care I know she will always be well taken care of. *Laughing* Look at me, I'm alive.

Shaking her head You and your morbid humor *and I'm kissed on the forehead.* I'll let you know when we are ready.

As Cynthia and Amanda leaves me to myself I review the documents once again. Trying to decipher who this person is and why me, I decide in a flick of a second to get all my questions answered directly. I will fly to New York and get an understanding of all of this myself. I'm flying home.

Chapter 12: New York

*I land at Westchester County Airport a bit after
noon. With no checked luggage I'm able to whisk
pass all lines and make my way to the car rental
area. After about a ten minute wait I'm face to face
with NY attitude. No smile, no good afternoon just*

How can I help you?

I would like to rent a car

Do you have a reservation?

No I don't

I don't know if we have anything *with eye rolling
and all*

I'll take whatever you have

Do you have a license?

*No ass, I'm going to rent and drive a car without
one.* Yes I do *pulling out my wallet*

You will need a major credit card too

Not a problem *and I pull both my license and
American Express Black Card from my wallet.
Accepting both in hand without even looking me in
the face, the woman begins entering data into the
computer. After about two minutes of typing she stops
looks up at me then says pleasantly* "One second Mrs.
Walker" *and walks off to another women at the end*

*of the long counter. After an exchange of words both
women return to where I stand. The other woman
now communicating with me*

Good afternoon Mrs. Walker what type of Vehicle
were you looking for?

Anything you have?

How long would you need the rental for?

*How do I say I don't know without looking like a
fool* Until Wednesday.

And you will be returning it here?

Ahh yes.

After about a five minute pause We do have a Jag
available.

A what?

Smiling a Jaguar

I really don't need anything elaborate. A simple
compact will do.

Are you sure?

Very

We do have a Ford Escort that just came in

That would do just fine

If you have a seat in the wait area, we will get it
prepped for you.

Thank you. *I make my way to the plush set of chairs. Concerned with if Cynthia found my note yet I pull my phone out to review any missed calls. So far none which means Kevin hasn't yet been told anything. I cringe at the thought of him being not only angry but worried. But this is something I must do on my own. Based on what I learned so far Kevin had no intent to tell me anything. Rather, handling it on his own and pretend all is well.*

Excuse me Mrs. Walker the car is ready.

Thank you. *I follow the gentleman to the escort parked right out front. Taking the keys* Thank you again.

Prior to pulling off I contemplate where I should go next. Agreeing with my inner voice I call 411 Hello could I have the address and telephone number for the Brooklyn District Attorney's Office.

****

Hello, how can I help you?

I'm not sure who is working on a case I'm involved with. My name is Elizabeth Walker.

Mrs. Walker do you have an appointment?

Here we go again. If I had an appointment I would know who to ask for No I don't have an appointment.

Have a seat and I will see if anyone can assist you.

Not sitting a good five minutes two gentlemen emerge from behind the guarded door and greet me.

Mrs. Walker I'm Brian Young kings County District Attorney and this is Andrew Keys Assistant District Attorney. It is a pleasure to finally meet you *Each extending their hands to shake mine.* Please follow me to my office.

Following as instructed we end at Brian Young's office.

Please have a seat.

Thank you

Mrs. Walker I'm glad to see you are doing well.

Yes I am

Based on my last conversation with your husband we assumed you were still under medical care?

My husband can be over protective Mr. Young. But I'm here now, in person to answer any questions and I hope you will do the same.

Certainly Mrs. Walker. Will Mr. Walker and Mr. Strickland be joining us?

Mr. Strickland?

Your attorney?

Confused Why do I need an attorney?

An equally confused look Mrs. Walker what do you know about this case.

Shaking my head Nothing.

What brings you here today Mrs. Walker?

Until this morning I assumed *choking back emotions trying to emerge* I assumed Karen Black was responsible for my kidnapping, for Rosie and Rosa's death. Responsible for all that has happened.

Sensing my building emotional state Mrs. Walker maybe we should wait for your husband?

Sounding now agitated by the suggestion No we will not. This is about me, about my life. I'm here now please tell me what is going on.

Mrs. Walker I reviewed your statement from when you were abducted. You stated you heard multiple voices.

Please don't make me go back to that time Yes I heard a woman crying and another laughing.

From what we learned your captures consisted of Angela Black, Olivia Jenkins and Tiffany Morris.

Olivia Jenkins? Tiffany Morris? Tiffany Morris, my ex-husband's daughter?

Yes and Olivia Jenkins, his step-daughter

Confused Why?

Mrs. Walker Olivia Jenkins confessed to your kidnapping and killing The Morales.

What? That can't be. Angela told me she killed Rosie and Rosa.

It seems Angela was involved but did not act alone.

I really don't understand. I thought Michael's daughters were missing?

That was our understanding also until your husband and his partner located their whereabouts.

Hesitating He what?

Mrs. Walker maybe

Interrupting Please I'm not fragile I can handle the information.

It seems Olivia and her sister were living with Angela Black. When the apartment was searched Olivia was found along with her sister.

What the fuck? And my husband knows correction knew about all of this?

Yes Mrs. Walker. We had been in communication with Mr. Walker primarily due to your health.

And they both confessed?

After the two lawyers exchange a look Mr. Yong answers No. Tiffany was unconscious when we found her. Olivia injected her with high levels of heroine.

A chill comes over me Like she did to me *I blurt out. Composing myself* Her sister, is she okay?

She is alive.

Why did Olivia do this to her own sister?

Your husband initiated an extensive background check on Olivia. It seems she has a history of psychiatric hospitalizations beginning at the age of seven.

For what?

Her diagnosis include Multiple Personality Disorder, Mood Disorder, Bi-Polar, Schizophrenia and that's only naming a few.

I'm sorry but I don't understand why me?

Not offering any information until now Mr. Keys explains The latest report details a tumultuous relationship between her mother and Michael Morris. She blames you for her mother's unhappiness, the domestic abuse her mother endured. She literally feels you are evil.

This sounds too familiar, Angelia said the same to me, blamed me for the abuse. She felt I could have prevented it.

Mr. Keys continues Olivia's hallucinations are fixed on you. The voices tell her you must die.

The words send a chill down my back

She had a plan to do it.

And that plan was Angela?

Not sure what Angela Black's role was but Olivia Jenkins wants and wanted you dead.

Overwhelmed by this information I begin to visibly shake

Mrs. Walker are you okay?

Trying to force a smile I am. Knowing that I can finally put this behind me.

The two exchange another look with one another Mrs. Walker unfortunately this case is nowhere close to being settled.

Mr. Young I don't understand. You have her in custody and she confessed.

Yes she has however her advocates and attorney feel she is not competent to stand trial.

An insanity plea?

More or less, yes

Well wouldn't that be accurate?

Not necessarily. At this time she is stable, coherent and medication compliant.

What's the difference? Either way she would be locked away.

A significant difference. If granted an insanity plea release is based on her mental stability rather than serving a sentence.

But if her mental health is the concern wouldn't it be in the interest of all if she was placed in a psychiatric facility and received the oversight and therapy she is in need of?

Mrs. Walker I reviewed this matter with your husband and it was agreed she should stand trial.

Feeling completely dismissed I feel my anger building from within Where is she now?

Bellevue Hospital prison ward.

Who are her supports? *Curious to know if Michael has had any contact*

The maternal grandmother.

Mr. Young what about Michael?

Exchanging yet another look with Mr. Keys. He's a man of many excuses and with each excuse he has distanced himself. The grandmother has been the only family involvement, petitioning the court to have her granddaughter committed rather than a prison incarnation.

And I can't say I disagree. From what I've been told today this woman - girl has significant issues that stem from childhood

Interrupting me, Mr. Key's offers his astute observation Yes and from that childhood a fixation to fatally harm you.

So what happens now?

A competency hearing is scheduled for Wednesday. Depending on the outcome, the trial will begin shortly after.

Has Rosa's family been informed?

Yes they have. *Pausing* Mrs. Walker unfortunately this hearing will bring the case back into the public eye. Are you physically and emotionally prepared for this?

I guess I will have to be, do I have a choice not to be?

Mr. Young answering Unfortunately no.

Standing Well I will have to be. Thank you both for seeing me.

Both Mr. Young and Mr. Keys rise to their feet

Mrs. Walker do you have a cell number we can reach you on?

Yes *writing the number on a post it note provided by Mr. Young.* What is the maternal grandmother's name?

Harriet Jenkins *Mr. Young shares*

She resides In North Carolina?

No Saddle River New Jersey *Mr. Young appearing concerned with my questions* Why Mrs. Walker?

Just curious. Well thank you both again.

Exiting the building, I stop just outside pulling out my cell phone. I call information Saddle River New Jersey Harriet Jenkins.......

Chapter 13: A Search For Truth

Before giving myself an opportunity to debate the decision to drive to Saddle River, New Jersey and acting without a plan I find myself sitting in my car right outside the home of a murder's grandmother. I know I haven't thought this through. How am I going to introduce myself? Hi I'm the woman your psychotic granddaughter tried to kill. You're the grandmother of the bitch who killed two special people. Yes I thought this out perfectly. And if I muster the strength to confront this woman where does it say she is obligated to talk to me? Why would she? Supporting a woman who has caused such horrendous pain – misery, shit why am I putting myself through this? No I made a mistake coming here today. Although I have a self-deprived need to know why me, why the people I loved I know it would be best to pull off and never look back.

Following through on my own recommendation I prepare myself to leave when suddenly I'm startled by a tap on my window. Looking up I find myself looking into the face – the eyes of a somewhat familiar face, the face of a woman I met many years ago at Michael's grandmother's home. I roll down my window.

You've been sitting at least 30 minutes. Did you come to see me?

Stuttering, I believe so Mrs. Jenkins

Then get out the car and follow me inside.

Uneasy with the request Mrs. Jenkins do you know who I am?

Certainly girl, I remember the first time we met on that Fourth of July. Yes I certainly know who you are.

I'm sorry I bothered you, coming here is a mistake.

The only mistake would be leaving without getting answers to the questions you have. *Gesturing for me to get out of the car* Come on child, nothing to be afraid of here.

I step out of the car and follow Mrs. Jenkins into her home.

Please have a seat anywhere.

Following direction I take a seat on the couch closer to the door I apologize for not calling before showing up at your door.

No apology needed, I'm just glad I am home to meet with you. How have you been doing?

Well thank you

Well huh...... I assume under such circumstances well would be an understatement. And the baby, healthy?

A daughter and yes she is doing well too.

Then my prayers for you were answered. Thank you Jesus.

Surprised You prayed for me?

I certainly did. I prayed for you, your husband and your baby. Prayed that you would have an opportunity to hold your precious child in your arms.

Tears begin to form Thank you...

Thanking me for a prayer is unnecessary *shaking her head.* So tell me why the need to see me?

Sighing deeply I.... I really don't know. The District Attorney informed me of your involvement with your granddaughter and next thing *I release a nervous laugh* I'm sitting outside your home.

I understand

Smiling I'm glad one of us does then. *Nervously rubbing my hands together* I was told you were pushing an insanity plea?

Yes I am

Do you...........

Do I what? *Her tone presenting stern*

I'm sorry

Listen I'm not blind to what my granddaughter has done. I know what she did and I know what she is capable of doing if not receiving the proper help. In prison she will not get the necessary psychiatric care she is desperately in need of.

Silence filling the air, my heart races. I fight the inner me from asking the 20 million dollar question. Battle lost and although meek and whimpering words are formed and verbalized Why me? Why the anger towards me? *Tears begin rolling down my cheeks.*

Looking me straight in the eyes and inhaling deeply Do you remember when we met?

Yes I do, we met at Michael's grandparent's home.

Yes. Up to that day I somewhat supported my daughter's relationship with Michael.

Why up to that day?

Elizabeth I've known Michael and his family even before Michael was born. His family and mine not close but certainly cordial, our homes side by side.

My late husband, a respected attorney often worked with Michael's grandfather representing his business ventures. When my husband passed my daughter only 12 at the time spiraled down. *Softening her voice* Karen *shaking her head* struggled to be accepted – validated. Nothing I did provided her with what she was looking for. By the age of fourteen she was heavy into drugs, became a heroine addict. She ran away from home so many times that I lost count. Each time found two and three days later in places you wouldn't let a dog stay. Oh how I prepared myself for that one dreaded phone call because I knew I would be burring my one and only child. I knew in my heart she wasn't going to see her eighteenth birthday. Then at the age of 17 she had Olivia. *Shaking her head* My granddaughter was damned before her birth with all that garbage Karen put into her system. But things began to change for the better. The more she saw Michael when he would drive down from New York to see his grandparents the more Karen got her life on track, eventually getting help with the drugs and staying clean. If for nothing else the hold he had over my baby back then saved her life. The only support she had was Michael and me. The closer the two of them got the more time he spent in North Carolina. Every chance he had he went down to see Karen and Olivia and during that time of kindness she fell in love with Michael. For many years the two were inseparable *Her voice changes to a displeasing tone* Then out of the blue the announcement of you and Michael's marriage.

Please understand. I did not know about Karen.

I believe you didn't. However Karen believed differently. She believed what she was told to her. You were pregnant and Michael was being forced to marry you by his family.

Forced?

Hmm, yes forced. See we are talking about the Carter's, the family of no wrong – the family with no breakable window panes. The family even to this day has a reputation to up hold. A prominent black family that the community looks up to. But when held in such high regards pebbles thrown tend to shatter windows.

I don't understand.

Child your pebble shattered their glass house.

That wasn't my intent.

That 4th of July when I met you, from that day the perfect life I thought my daughter had came to light. I saw the hell she put herself into and what she had my granddaughter apart of. She knew Olivia already had challenges but *shaking her head* what that girl seen.

What do you mean?

When you left that evening I saw the fire in his eyes. The embarrassment for his family, the wife he said he left and was divorcing pops up at a family gathering as if life was perfect.

Until that evening I thought it was.

So did my daughter, in her mind. But you physically being present showed her life was so very different. She confronted Michael after you left and of course he made every excuse imaginable. After giving her and Michael a few minutes of privacy I went in to check on them both. When I did I walked in to find Michael holding Karen forcibly and tight, his eyes spitting fire. When I inquired what was going on he turned back on that arrogant charm stating Karen was upset and he was just calming her down. I knew better asking Karen again privately but she just dismissed me.

Shortly after that evening I started seeing changes in Olivia's behavior, fighting anyone and everyone, cussing and *trying to hold back tears* saw her hit her baby sister with such force. Tiffany wasn't even a year old at the time.

Was injured?

From the outside, no. But many incidents took place after. My final breaking point was Jasmine's birth, that unforgettable Thanksgiving.

Seeing the pain on my face Yes that Thanksgiving. Karen just didn't go into labor that evening, that bastard pushed my daughter to the ground during an argument. Initially Karen told me she slipped but Olivia told it all, witnessing not only that time but many times before. That evening I took Karen to the hospital and I was the one who helped her in the delivery room because that bastard was nowhere to be found. It wasn't until the next morning when his mother stopped by the hospital to explain what had happened to you. She wanted Karen to hear it from her – from family rather than hearing from the media. I would say that day started the many dark days I was going to experience.

Unable to suppress my curiosity What was she told?

Michael went by the house and found you. Oh and the baby did not belong to Michael.

Shaking my head I have no words.

Your sister certainly cleared things up. You and Karen were in the same hospital, same floor. After Paulette told us what had happened I tried to see what information I could get on my own. Luck would have it, I overheard your sister putting Paulette in her place. It was during that discussion that all the pieces to the puzzle were in place, the picture complete. I returned to my daughter's room and shared what I just learned. I told her I was packing her and the girls things and we all were returning to New Jersey. She refused and I told her I was not going to support any of the nonsense any longer, I couldn't. I offered to take Olivia with me and she refused. I left the hospital that day, returned to NJ and didn't return until having to first bury my granddaughter then to bury my only child.

I'm so sorry.

Don't be. I know she is finally at peace and that bastard living in his own hell. He is the cause of all of this.

But I don't understand why your granddaughter is fixated on me?

Initially my daughter despised you because of the hold she felt you had on Michael. As the years passed I believe she became envious of you.

Envious, why – For what?

You stood on your two feet and walked away.

I wouldn't say that is completely accurate.

You walked away from that bastard and never looked back. My baby girl regardless how hard I tried to tell her differently, regardless how hard and often he hurt her she couldn't leave. Till the day she left this earth he had a hold – power over her. She stayed with that man even after knowing he had a family with another woman. Now you asked me why Olivia is fixated on you. Beyond her emotional challenges imagine seeing your mother hit, beat, humiliated day after day. Seeing your mother getting high after being clean for so many years. Imagine being loved and adored until the man who said he loved you like his own had his own. Imagine hearing about another woman who tore your family apart. *Shaking her head* That's why. *Her voice cracking* I knew from the first time she tried to harm Tiffany I knew something was wrong. Then the hallucinations and voices. As she got older the outburst became more intense. At one point it was suggested she remain in a residential setting and my daughter disagreed.

Thinking of the pending case Maybe you shouldn't be telling me this.

Why I have nothing to hide. What I'm telling you is what I shared with the District Attorney with hopes of having his support to place her in a psychiatric facility where she will finally get the help she desperately needs. I don't want to see her released, I have Tiffany to consider. What Olivia put Tiffany through since being birthed into this world is unimaginable.

Where is Tiffany now?

Saint Agatha's. When she and Olivia were found at that Black's woman's home, Tiffany had been injected with high doses of heroine. She also suffered a brain hemorrhage due to being hit with a blunt object.

Oh….

Yes and Olivia admits to it all. *Tears falling down her face* I know what she did and I'm not making excuses for her nor her behaviors but she is my granddaughter. I failed her mother and I can't fail her too. She needs help and I will do whatever has to be done to insure she gets the proper help.

What the hell is wrong with me? I'm sitting here feeling empathy for the sick bitch that tried to kill me not once but twice? Shake it Beth, do not give in.

What is Michael's involvement now?

He saw Tiffany once in three months. His mother, grandparents not even a phone call. They can't face that all this is his fault. But I would rather they stayed away. My granddaughters and I don't need the toxicity in our lives. They – we are better off without them.

Before I could understand my need to have it the words slip out Do you have a number for Michael?

With a wary look Why for peak sake do you need it?

Honestly I'm not sure. I flew home today to seek some type of closure and I think he will be the only person to give it to me.

Sweet girl why put yourself through that? *Standing and walking into the kitchen, Mrs. Jenkins returns with her address book.* If you must *opening her phone book, writing the number on a piece of paper* here is his cell.

Standing now Thank you for meeting with me. I really do appreciate it.

I hope I was able to provide you with some helpful information.

You did, you really did. Thank you again and I hope everything works out for both of your granddaughters.

Thank you *hugging me* Take care of yourself and your family.

I will *stepping out of the door the wheels begin spinning. The only person that can give me the closure I'm looking for is from Michael himself.*

Chapter 14: Plan or No Plan

From New Jersey to New York, from Saddle River to Rockland the same question asked with no returned answer, will I really contact Michael? With all that I learned in the few hours I've been back in New York I have a need like never before to ask him directly "why" and this need can only be met if done in person –face to face – eye to eye. But with this need I feel an uneasiness with myself. Meeting with Michael presents as a level of disloyalty to my husband to my daughter to my family. Sitting here in front of my home, outside the secured gate that is to protect us from the evils and threats I find difficulty entering. The thoughts filling my head – the plan I'm piecing together to insure I have my time with Michael I question if I'm worthy to be in a place I call home with my husband.

Debating no longer I enter the code that allows my entrance and drive up and around to the back of the house. As if sneaking around I park as far into the back as possible. Walking from the back to the front of the house I take in the beauty of my home. From the droplets of icicles hanging from the bare trees to the frozen water of the Hudson River claiming the last rays of today's winter sun. Being in Texas for as long as I had, I forgot the beauty of a New York winter's day.

I step into my beautiful empty home turning on only the light in the foyer. I head directly upstairs to the nursery and take a seat in the familiar rocker. I need to surround myself with material objects that represent my precious gem. I need this to give me the strength to make this call. I need it to help me face the wrath that awaits. Pull it together Beth, you know what needs to happen. The one person who could answer that million dollar question is Michael himself. No peace will come to you until you do. With shaking hands and an accelerated heartbeat I step out of the pure sterile environment of my daughter's room and into the hallway. I inhale deeply and make the call. After several rings Michael's voice mail picks up.

Ahh hi Michael. Um I really need to talk to you. Could you please call me back as soon as you can? I would really appreciate it, thanks. *All I can do now is wait. I return to my bedroom and stretch across my bed. A smile surfaces as my thoughts think of Kevin and his touch but the imaginable thought of his touch is replaced with the thought of him being concerned – worried about me. As the tears begin to fall I close my eyes and give into the darkness that welcomes me in.*

****

Ms. Black how are you today?

………..

Ms. Black is everything okay?

………..

What is it?

He took a piece of me every day since the first day we met.

Who? What was taken from you?

He took my beauty, my health, my love for life and my humanity. All that was left was a hollow shell.

Ms. Black – Angela who took this from you? How did they?

My soul is unworthy and I'm no longer pure. He did this to me and I let him. He did this to me.

Please turn to me, look at me please.

I finally found love. Yes a love like no other, a love rarely shared. I loved – I loved – I loved.

Ms. Black who are you referring to?

And even then he snatched my happiness, leaving me all alone.

You're not alone, I'm here with you.

The one person who understood me, took me in and loved me unconditionally. The one person who loved me and my children. The person who saved me is the one I turned on, How could I?

Ms. Black I'm trying to understand

Finally acknowledging she's not alone, You don't understand? *Her tone calm but accusatory* You better than anyone should understand, the puppet master herself you understand.

....

Pulling, tugging and manipulating that's what you do. Michael was right, an evil bitch to the core.

What did I do to you?

The question shouldn't be what you've done but what you didn't do.

Confused, hurt and lost all that I am feeling. My tone changes completely, my words loud and meaningful What do you want me to do? What should I do?

Turning away from me You could have stopped all the hurt and pain a long time ago. Because you didn't my death, Karen, that pretty baby and her mother all dead because of you. The blood shed is all because of you. Until you understand what needs to be done damnation will be your only salvation.

Angela… Ms. Black Just tell me what I did, what I should have done. Please tell me and I will do it. *Fading from my sight Please* don't go, I don't understand….. Please don't go.

Awaken from a familiar disturbing sleep I immediately jump up and turn on the light. Reminding myself of where I'm at and my need for answers I search for my cellphone that is ringing continually. Found at my side I look at the number hoping to be anyone but Kevin and as luck would have it, the caller is Kevin. About to answer the ringing stops and the house phone rings. Picking up after the second ring, I brace myself.

Hello

Beth *his tone calm but abrasive* what are you doing?

Kevin everything is okay. I'm fine.

Erickson is on his way. He will pick you up and fly back to Texas with you.

No do not send Erickson. I have a few things to take care of, once I'm done I will head back.

Hearing his building anger What do you need to take care of?

Kevin I'm fine. Trust me I can take care of myself.

Trust you? Huh Beth stop the bullshit your flying back tonight.

He hit a trigger Stop the bullshit? Is that how you see it? My life is bullshit? I'm a grown ass woman

Interrupting me Then act like a grown ass woman. Beth you told me you understood, you told me you would follow the rules and although you say you're *his tone raising* a grown God Damn woman you're acting like a fucking child sneaking around. You gave me your word.

And you gave me yours. You told me you would treat me like an equal and never keep anything from me. Huh funny how that worked out.

Softening his voice And I did just that.

Really? I met with the Brooklyn DA today. Nice to know you and he had conversations that involved me, making decisions that could affect me.

Beth...

Don't. You can't keep me in a bubble. I've told you over and over again I have to get through this in my own way in my own time.

Beth we will work through this together.

No Kevin I have to take care of this on my own.

What do you need to take care of?

Kevin I just need time, please can't you understand that?

Beth do you know what threats are out there?

Kevin I'll be fine. Amanda is well taken care of

Raising his voice I know my daughter is taken care of. It is your ass I'm worried about. Beth I'm not playing any of your games. Erickson will be there shortly.

Please don't send anyone for me, I just need a day or so. *Not giving him an opportunity to debate with me* Kevin I love you, make sure my daughter knows I love her too. I will call the house in the morning to explain to Cynthia, all will be fine. As I place the house phone back onto its cradle my cell begins to ring.

Hello

………. Beth I received your message.

Thank you for calling me back. *Pausing for a few seconds* Michael I've been thinking about you – us a lot lately.

Why?

If I knew I wouldn't had called you. I was wondering if we could meet.

Meet with who?

Just you and me, no one else.

You caught my attention.

I'll come to you?

I just flew into JFK and have to head upstate to Marlborough for an early morning meeting.

I know a perfect place we could meet about 20 minutes from Marlborough. I could meet you about 8:30?

That should give me enough time.

Then meet me at the Muddy River off route 9.

Should I secure a hotel room for you? I wouldn't want you driving back so late.

Son of a bitch, should I really be surprised? Worrying about me traveling late really! No let me take care of that. I'll see soon then. *Hanging up the phone I notice the time, already 6:30. I grab my purse then head down to leave. Passing Kevin's study I'm reminded of what is kept in his safe. Without a second thought I open the safe and retrieve my possession. Prepared now, I leave the place I considered my safe haven, my home to meet with the man who brought me to my breaking point. Who as of this minute seems to have that same hold over me as he had over Karen and*

Angela. Our similarities – the need for his companionship. Our differences – my need to understand why, my need for him to pay for what he has done to me.

Chapter 15: Driving To The Truth

After what seems like the most intense drive of my life I finally make it to my destination. Strategizing my need to get answers from Michael I decided to communicate in an environment he has come accustom to doing business in. Pulling into a sleazy local hotel I make my way inside.

Well how can I help you this evening?

A room please.

Looking around me, solo are we?

Yes, would you have an available room?

I'm sure I have something for you *said with a dirty implied smile. After looking at me from the floor up several times* Yes I do. That would be $38.50.

Handing the country redneck my cash, my hand is rubbed then squeezed. I forcefully pull away, take the key from the counter and head to room 5. Fleeing in some sense, my struts are both fast but filled with furry. How dare the asshole? Before I know it I'm standing outside room five. Fumbling with the key with my shaking hands I finally unlock the door. Opening the door I realize if I step in I will not come out, I will not be able to follow through on my plans.

It would be my excuse to avoid what – who needs to be confronted. Shutting the door immediately I head across the road to The Muddy River, a honky tonk - bluesy bar. The place I asked Michael to meet me, the place where my confronting him will begin.

Entering I'm immediately reminded of my last time here - about three years ago. Attending a three day conference in the nearby town a group of us in from the city decided to have a night out. We were told the Muddy River would provide us with the entertainment we were looking for. To our surprise we indeed enjoyed the live band and strangely enough the country rednecky atmosphere. Entering now I find that very little has changed. Still dark, smoky, dreary and off the beaten path. This scene is exactly what I'm looking for this evening. I step in and take a seat at a table located not too far from the door. A waitress greeting me as I sit.

Hi, can I get you something?

A beer please.

Staring at me for a few seconds the redheaded waitress smiles politely Hey just want to warn you, this place will be packed in about twenty minutes. Be a bit weary we get all types.

I guess my appearance presents as if I shouldn't be in a place like this. Thanks.... I know some of the types *smiling* I've been here a few times before. *Playing it off as though I was more of regular but by her expression she knows better.* But that wasn't recent, last time was about three years ago.

Oh, then what took you so long to come back?

Should I tell the truth I don't make my way from the city all that often.

Smiling Well then welcome back *and she walks away assuming to retrieve my beer. As she departs promptly at 8:30 Michael arrives dressed in business attire wearing a tailored suit and wing tip shoes. Catching the eyes of the few women here he flashes that cocky smile. A tall thin brunette waitress presenting herself smiles largely at him. Yes ladies tall, dark and a tight body. Yup handsome he is on the outside but pure darkness – evil in the inside.*

Seeing him walk through the door turns my stomach completely. I try to contain my panic as he immediately zooms in on me and walks over while shining that annoying smile. From the pit of my stomach I feel consumed with nausea.

Well hello Elizabeth

Michael.... Please have a seat. *Attempting to kiss me on my lips I turn immediately for my cheek to be the receiver.*

Aren't We far from the well-lit path? *said with pure sarcasm*

Hmm….. How was your drive up?

Long but knowing I was seeing you *rubbing my arm* made it well worth the drive.

Just in time to interrupt the king of all bull shitters the waitress returns Here you go *placing my beer on the table. Turning to Michael* Can I get you something?

Not taking his eyes off me and continuing to rub my arm I'll have corona with lime and a shot of tequila.

Needing a more potent liquid encourager myself I too request a shot. Please make that two shots

Sure. Coming right up

Look how you've grown up. Tequila huh!

Only if he knew, I will need more than one shot to get through this night - to stomach his companionship his touch. Sitting with him this very moment continues to be the cause of my stomach's acrobatic abilities. Yes I guess I have.

Well you look... Good

Hmm

Once again impeccable timing Here you go *and the two shots are placed on the table along with the Corona. I hand the waitress a 100.00 bill folded while looking directly in her eyes.* Please keep the shots coming.

Exchanging a "jackpot" look after opening her hand Sure thing.

So you needed to talk to me in person?

Yes I did. Lately I find myself thinking about our relationship.

What is there to think about?

Why it didn't work out.

With a stone cold look It didn't work out because of you.

Did this fucking man just let that come out his mouth? No I heard wrong Excuse me?

His eyes cold and hard I didn't stutter. *Shrugging his shoulders*

You just got your answer. My fault huh, in an instant I feel my anger building. Calm down Beth. His pathetic cocky ass just solidified your reason for inviting him here. Hold it together. Playing it off to the best of my ability I ignore his blinded view of our past and inquire about the present.

Everyone doing well?

As best as one could expect. What about you? Still together with the cop?

He's pushing every fucking button I have Yes I am. Dare I ask who you are with these days?

Just doing me

Bet you are insensitive bastard How long will you be here in New York?

I'm scheduled to fly back tomorrow after my meeting.

How is the family business?

Surviving. Of course not to the level that your man seemed to have stumble into.

I can take the jabs at me but I can't take the blatant disrespect toward Kevin Listen can you please stop with the insults?

I can't control how you interpret what I say.

Really Michael! You know this was a mistake *Rising to my feet my hand is taken and I'm pulled back down into my seat*

Why are we here Elizabeth?

Cut the shit with the Elizabeth thing. Yes my name but the only time I'm called by full name by you is when you were trying to fuck me. I exhale loudly What?

This little get together, you could have told me what you needed to by phone.

I told you already, I've been thinking more about you – us and what we did or did not have.

And why is that. You finally realized what you had?

Ignoring his arrogant son of a bitch comment No more so to get some type of closure for us both, you and me.

Leaning into me Closure from me? I told you long ago we have a connection that can never be broken.

A cold chill cascades down my back Humph

Humph what? *Appearing displeased with my response.*

Just as it sounded.

Where's your man anyway? I'm sure he would disapprove with *tilting his head and leaning into me* you having a need to talk to me.

Do you really want to talk about him?

Not really, at this point in time he is....
Insignificant.

Beth do not Lose it. He's just trying to push your buttons. But deep down I know better, the arrogant son of a bitch sitting across from me really believes he's the be all and end all, God's greatest creation to the human race. I sigh involuntarily, chug now my second shot to his fourth. I scan for the waitress who is nowhere to be seen. Desperately needing another shot of liquid encouragement I once again attempt to stand.

Once again grasping my arm Where are you going?

I don't see our waitress, I'm going to order us another round then maybe we should go.

With the fucking cocky - arrogant grin Whatever you say.

I make my way to the bar and order two more shots. Presented with no time like the present I hover at the end of the low lit bar and sprinkle my special something into Michael's drink. Waiting a few seconds for the powder residue to settle I head back to the table. Here you go *handing Michael his drink*

So where are we going?

My Surprise Michael. Don't worry it will be worth your while. *Just as I'm reassuring Michael the house band begins to play a Blusey version of Wade In The Water. The alcohol now my guider I stand and extend my hand to Michael* Dance with me.

You don't dance

Part of my growth, I do now *the lies just keep flowing. Michael stands and follows me onto the dance floor which is packed and forces our body to body contact. With both hands on my hips we begin swaying to the beat. Stroking me from my mid-section* sides to *my hips I'm turned to where my back is against him. In this moment reality sets in. Am I really going to do this? Feeling his manhood erected and against me tears begin to form. I swallow hard and continue my solicitous dance.*

Whispering in my ear I think we need to be on our way.

Hesitantly I nod my head in agreement. Walking from the dance floor to where we were sitting Michael Stumbles a bit

Are you okay?

Never better

Making our way to the door Maybe I should drive?

No one drives my car but me.

Material things still take priority huh

What did you say *as if not comprehending*

Let's get going

Where are we going to?

Just across the highway. We could walk if you like?

Presenting dizzy Here *giving me the keys* scratch it and it will be your ass!

Now it feels like old times Don't worry your precious car will be just fine.

Michael Stumbles into the passenger seat barely able to maintain his balance. As I Climb into the driver's seat I notice his second passion - love, his golf clubs sitting perfectly in the back. Shaking my head I confirm what I already knew, nothing changed with this bastard. Always driving a Mercedes or a BMW, always insuring he had the best golfing gear – attire and playing at the best courses yet the people- hell his children, Angelia's kids not being taken care of? Her and the children living in a shelter, depending on others to feed and take care of them all.

Tears begin to form as I allow myself to revisit that time in my life when I lived with no utilities not because he didn't have the money but his way of punishing me.

Pulling myself from my own thoughts I drive approximately 1/2 Mile and make a u turn - ending at the motel. Getting out the car I'm grabbed forcefully and pinned against the car.

I've been waiting too long for this night, I'm going to enjoy every second.

Hmm yes, yes you will *and I release myself from his hold. We enter the 4 by 4 sleazy stale smoke smelling room. Michael presenting even more so disoriented sits on the bed and motions for me to come to him. Before I could inquire what he wants I'm grabbed and pulled down to him to be kissed. Pulling away I'm pulled by my ponytail. What the fuck did I get myself into.* Michael slow down we have all night.

And I'm going to take what's mine the whole fucking night. *His words hit from within and I push myself away from his grasp.*

Oh you want to play, so be it.

Michael *trying to remain calm,* why the rush?

Stop the bullshit. Take your clothes off

We have all night

Either you will or I will

Beginning to panic I sit on the edge of the bed to take off my shoes trying to delay as much as possible.

Fuck this *and immediately Michael is on top of me grasping at my breast.*

No stop

Ignored completely my blouse is ripped open

Michael stop *and with all my strength I push him off*

His words slurring bitch your ass is mine *then complete silence.*

Finally out cold I drag Michael to the middle of the floor and handcuff his hands together. I then tie his legs together with rope. Sitting on the edge of the bed I begin to organize my thoughts. Looking down at *myself, my blouse torn open and my breast exposed I immediately feel sick to my stomach. I promised myself I would never let this man touch me again and I allowed it. I feel so dirty, violated. I feel as if I betrayed the one man I love with all I have. The thought of Michael touching me more I jump up and fully clothed step into the shower. I try to wash his stench his touch off me, scrubbing harder and harder. I shower in my clothes refusing even in his drunken - Rupeed state to give any sense of having me.*

After an hour or so of allowing the cascading droplets to cleanse me, dripping wet I come out the shower – out of the bathroom and stand over Michael. Playing out in my head what I was going to do to this bastard. I play back in my mind the pain and hurt I will inflict as he had on me. My day of retribution and retaliation has finally come. But standing here I decide to retrieve one of his golf clubs from his car. Why? Unsure this moment but with certainty will be used.

Returning to the room, Michael remains still – dead to the world. I take a seat just in front of him and wait for him to once again be alert and ready to play.

Chapter 16: The Truth of it All

Startled by my left cheek being caressed I open my eyes to Michael standing right in front of me. Shit I must have fallen asleep. Fuck, what am I going to do?

Into games I see

Michael I

Shh *placing his fingers over my lips.* You just made this much more interesting.

I need to go, I need to go right now!

After we take care of this tension that seems to be between us, then you can leave. Right now we are going to make love like we use to.

No *attempting to stand*

Shoved forcefully back down Oh no, I'm in control of this, of you. You will do what I say and when.

I'm sorry this was a mistake

Yes it was *said with a look I begged God not see in my life again.* You couldn't even put handcuffs on the right way. What the fuck have you ever done correct in your life?

Michael please let's just call it an evening.

The evening is just getting started.

Attempting to stand again I'm smacked across the face. I jump immediately back up Fucking bastard don't touch me again.

Or what? *with a large smile* Who is coming to rescue you, your man? Hmmm maybe he will find you but based on the voice messages he's been leaving you, he has no idea where you are or who you are with.

He has my cell? Please – oh I hope I left it outside my purse. Eyeing my purse on the chair beside me I snatch it immediately and look inside. Michael now sitting on the edge of the bed laughing.

Are you looking for this? *Holding the pistol I retrieved from Kevin's safe.* Elizabeth what were your plans? *Shaking his head* You don't have it in you to pull the trigger so I would assume you brought it with you to use as a prop. *Forcefully pulling my face up to look into his eyes* right?

………..

Answer me *Anger building in his voice*

Michael please just let me go, I'm sorry please..

Taking off his suit jacket Now Elizabeth you asked to see me for a reason.

I told you, I need closure.

And I told you, no goodbyes. We have a bond for life and I've been waiting patiently for this day to come.

My voice shivering and low We don't have a bond.

Pulling me up to him Oh we do *with his fingers he begins stoking my breast.*

Please don't do this, please *pushing him away with all my strength*

Angering him even more by my rejection I'm pushed against the wall with my arms pinned above me. Breathing hard his warm breathe flows over me beginning at my lips then my breast. Fighting to release myself from his hold my right hand slips from his grasp and I repeatedly smack his face, his chest any area I can make contact with. But my attempts of getting him off me leads to his accelerated excitement. Pushed to the bed my blouse is ripped off completely. I beg through my loud screaming cries to stop, but no response. His eyes cold, hard and looking through me rather than at me.

Unbuttoning my pants I continue to fight, kick and scream. Not phasing him at all my pants torn and pulled down. Unzipping his own he is now exposed.

The sight of his manhood and what is about to be I scream at the top of my lungs. My response an open hand across my face and a pillow to muffle anything further. My head fills with the faces of my baby girl and husband. I eternally ask for Kevin's forgiveness and brace myself for Michael's entrance into me. I hold my breath, still myself and think only of my husband, thinking of that morning I told him we were having a baby. The excitement written all over his face. Yes this is the image I will keep. But heavenly father I just ask that this is quick, please God I beg. My weeping is harder than before I lay and wait.

Beth are you okay?

Beth?

Being shaken I realize I'm no longer being held down, the pillow no longer on my face. I open my eyes to…… It can't be – but it is, my husband once again saves me.

Kevin I'm sorry so very sorry, please forgive me.

Baby are you okay?

Whispering I, did he *frozen in place* Did he?

Pulling me up into his arms I hold on to my man so tight. Please don't ever let me go, hold onto me forever, please.

Looking directly into my eyes I see only anger. Nothing at all behind the attentive attention he gives me in this moment. Responding to my request sounding compassionate but sterile After I take care of a small matter I will never let you go again. *Releasing me from his hold Kevin takes off his shirt and puts it on me. Just noticing that I sit bare breasted.* Erickson is going to take you out to the car *and from his words I now notice Erickson and Charles across the room hovering over Michael, each looking as angry as Kevin.*

No please don't leave me.

It will only be for a few minutes

Standing now I look down at my torn jeans that lay at my feet. I also see my panties still up and around me. Thank you God. Kevin immediately helps me pull my pants up to my waist.

Kevin I'm okay, I can do this

Laughing, Your wife, your woman shit the mother of your child came to me. How does that make you feel?

....

Shut up, just shut up *yelling from the top of my voice.*

Look at your man, he knows the truth.

Kevin please don t listen to him, please don't.

Erickson take her out now.

Oh did I hit a nerve Detective Walker?

No longer concerned with Kevin's anger. I'm about to explode. I break from Kevin's soft hold and without skipping a beat I pick up the pistol Michael neglected to retain. In a flash I point the gun directly at Michael.

Beth give me the gun *Kevin request in a soften voice*

I can't

Baby you can. Please give me the gun

Ignoring Kevin I calmly address Michael What have I ever done to you? What?

Beth don't do this, baby put down the gun

Kevin, I need you and everyone else but this useless bastard to leave now. You can't be here, I don't want you here!

I'm not going anywhere baby. Put the gun down.

He has caused some much pain.

He has baby.... But you have too much to live for to have it all taken away because of him. Think of our daughter, she needs her mother. She needs you to give her all that you wanted from a mother. Don't take that away from her.

Kevin he has to pay

He will every day of your happiness inflicts an internal pain within him baby. He feeds off your unhappiness and if the fire isn't fueled he will only have himself to destroy.

He's taken so much from me, he *laughing with tears falling* you *struggling to say how I feel* you were supposed to be my saving grace. You were supposed to keep me safe. You were to share a love with me that I never experienced. All this you was supposed to do, what you promised me. But instead you took soo much from me. You snatched my innocence and destroyed my dignity. You made me become something, someone I didn't want to be... I became a person that took an innocent life. I did that because of you.

I'm sorry

I'm not looking for an apology, just tell my why? To continue to live my life I need to know why? Why me? Because I was weak? Easy to manipulate? S*creaming* What? Did you even love me? Just tell me why?

I don't know Beth.

My trusted knight, my knight and shining protector, you're a coward a fucking coward.

And you an unwanted bitch that wanted everything and gave little.

You sick fuck, I wanted nothing from you but your love and I gave you everything I had down to my soul.

A soul? Lifeless bitch

Looking over to Kevin I see he is about to explode

Beth it is time to go.

I told you I'm not going anywhere until I have closure.

Baby we are done here, please give me the gun.

Listen to your man.

Michael please, why?

Why? Because

Because *I chuckle through my cry* because is your only response huh! Congratulations your response just confirmed you are your father's son. You not only succeeded but exceeded at becoming the person you despised the most. You are certainly your father's son.

Shut your fucking mouth

Laughing Now did I hit a nerve?

Just because your dressed in you designer digs underneath your still that unwanted bitch!

Fore once his insults not phasing me. The same ole Michael *and I laugh*

Speak to your mother lately?

And the uneasiness that was holding me back suddenly unleashed. He awoke that one trigger that will and has brought me to my breaking point. Kevin knowing this weakness walks directly in front of Michael

Kevin Move

Baby give me the gun. This piece of shit is not worth this. Think of our daughter.

And my thoughts immediately focus onto my baby girl. *Handing Kevin his gun I stare intensely at Michael* I've never felt the hate I have for anyone as I feel and have for you right this moment.

Your one weak pathetic woman

From his words immediately Kevin pounces onto Michael. Erickson and Charles doing very little to stop it.

Yelling Kevin stop… please stop

Finally pulling the two apart Michael remains in place with a nasty smirk. The reality is you couldn't pull the trigger. You will never let me go, never!

He can't be serious. I begin to laugh as I walk across the room to retrieve his golf club. Laughing out loud You're one hundred percent correct, I couldn't pull the trigger on anyone but I can allow you to feel the pain I once felt *and with all my strength I swing the club as forcibly as I can and hit Michael directly on his right side. His need to gasp for air confirms my contact.*

You fucking bitch, you will die for this.

Making my way to his left side another on point contact. I can do this all night.

Then you better kill me

Ahhh is that a threat? Hope not because it's rather a promise

Yelling as loud as one can after being hit with such force You yellow bitch

I think you have me confused with your mother.

Shut your fucking mouth.

Another soft spot huh. It must be devastating, the woman everyone says I resemble is finally preventing you from having your way. *And in this moment it hits me, I remind him of the best and worst of his life* I remind you of your mother. I remind you of the one women you say you love with all you have but hate just the same? *Realizing as I confront this bastard* After every beating after every derogatory word said to me you always followed the apology with the same statement "Two women I love most in the world are the two women who brings me to my breaking point"

....

All these years, your mother? Our likeness in looks always a brunt of a joke... "Your marrying a younger version of your mom" wow. Each slap, punch - kick? All because of her? *This sick son of a bitch....* You couldn't disrespect your mother but her look alike you could. You fucking sick son of a bitch.

You don't know what the fuck you're talking about.

I don't? All this time and the pieces fall into place. The obedient son you presented to be, so perfect could never rebel against the love of his life... No, but easily done to the women who presents as a photocopy. Wow....

Shut the fuck up.

All that you said you wouldn't be you became! Your father cheated, had children from multiple women and of course the biggest similarity beat his wife consistently. But to the world all that could be seen was the perfect son - the perfect family. It all makes sense.

....

Your misery.... Your misery

....

Handing Kevin the golf club Baby I'm sorry.....

While hugging me tight, Erickson and Charles rush in from where they have been standing like statues and begin tending to Michael.

Baby let's get home to our beautiful daughter.

Before we go I have one more matter to take care of

What?

Taking the golf club back I'll be right back *and with the golf club in hand I head outside and begin busting out every single window in Michael's car. I hit repeatedly everywhere leaving dents on top of dents. How wonderful this feels. When I walk back inside the look of surprise on everyone's face especially Michael's.*

You *standing directly in Michael's face* you are a pitiful excuse for a man. Up to now I didn't understand how I could have stopped you long ago. I didn't understand why you felt we had / have a bond. *Laughing with renewed tears streaming down my cheeks* I got it now, I could have stopped you a long time ago by putting you in jail for the abuse and raping me. If I had all that happened wouldn't have been. Lives would have been saved. As to this so called bond – hold, you have it twisted. You don't want me you just want to prove to your self-stimulating ego that no one leaves you *screaming* no one leaves but guess what I did. I left and never looked back. Get help you sick – sick bastard, get help. *Turning to Kevin* I'm ready to go home to Texas to my daughter now.

I happen to have a plane waiting to make that happen.

Walking to the car Are you okay?

With you in my life by my side I am perfect. But I will be even better once I'm home in Texas with you, my daughter and our family.

Chapter 17: Welcome Home

Mama... Mama...

Baby Happy Easter *Pulling myself up to a sitting position my eyes are greeted by my most treasured people. My ever so handsome husband and my beautiful baby girl.* Hey you two what are you up to?

Just wanted to give you your surprise from the Easter Bunny.

Smiling at Kevin Really? The Easter Bunny gave me exactly what I wanted last night.

And the Easter Bunny can't wait to give you some more *we both laugh.* But for now for you my love.

I accept the notable blue box from Tiffany's and open it. Baby.... I love it.

Just a physical reminder that you have the key to my heart.

And you have mine *Kissing my handsome husband*

Mandy give mommy her present..

More Kevin?

Something from Mandy and me...

Opening now my second blue box A Lockett *I open to find a picture of Kevin and my Amanda Rose*

Baby girl that's you and daddy. Thank you *kissing them both* And I know exactly what will go on the other side.

What?

Give me one minute *Climbing out of bed I walk into my closet and return with a large basket in hand.*

For me? *Kevin's eyes light up*

Yes but what do you get a man that has practically everything and can afford anything?

Anything and everything I've ever wanted is right here with me now.

Well then I hope this *taking an envelope from the basket and handing it to Kevin* will at least put a smile on your face

Opening the envelope the smile disappears immediately from Kevin's face. My heart sinks. Kevin?

I won't risk it.

No risk I promise. I'm fit as a fiddle.

Beth are you sure you want to do this and now?

I don't think we have a choice and I couldn't want anything more than this.

Oh baby *Kevin picks up Amanda and shows her the sonogram picture* you're going to be a big sister.

Amanda not understanding but by the smile on her face her dad holding and twirling her is all she needs to comprehend at this time.

Kevin stop twirling her *laughing* before her breakfast and God knows whatever else you allowed her to eat from her basket comes back up.

Daddy more, More

No more Mandy…. Mommy is right. *Kevin picks up the phone*

Who are you calling?

Mrs. Clarke *who answers on the firs ring* Could you come up and dress Mandy for Church? … Thank you.

Kevin I can get her ready?

No, neither of us can *and just then Mrs. Clarke appears.*

Could you dress Mandy for church?

Of course Kevin *smiling at both of us. I know she suspects and by the commotion no longer a suspicion.*

As Mrs. Clarke leaves with Amanda, Kevin takes me by the hand and leads me into the bathroom, turning on the shower. Taking off his own tank and night pants I am assisted with taking off my shorts and tee shirt and led into shower. The only words spoken are from Kevin whispering in my ear how blessed he is. With the click of the remote the sounds of Marvin Gaye and Tammi Terrell singing Your Precious Love fills the air. In sync with Kevin I sway to the beat and like all times before when sung to by him my knees go weak. I close my eyes and take in every word as the water cascades down upon us and his warm arms wrapped around me. Although singing to me right this moment, he assumes that I'm his saving grace but Tammi's words in this song expresses how he has saved me.

And I, I've got a song to sing

Tellin' the world about the joy you bring

And you gave me a reason for livin'

And ooo, you taught me, you taught me the meaning
of givin'

I thank God for sending this man into my life because he certainly was sent from above. Whispering in my ear

Every day there's something new

Honey, to keep me lovin' you

And with every passin' minute

Ah baby, so much joy wrapped up in it

What you've given me I could never return

'Cause there's so much, girl, I have yet to learn

As the song ends, I'm turned to face Kevin.
Stroking my left cheek with his other hand around my
waist You are truly the Center of my universe Mrs.
Walker. Since meeting, you have given me my
beautiful, beautiful daughter, our soon to be *touching*
my belly and taking my hand and placing it over his
heart giving me a will and purpose. I will always be
forever grateful, forever yours, forever my Beth Mrs.
Walker. You're my forever.

****

As we pull into the parking lot an uneasy feeling
sets in. The cheery excited mood established this
morning was slipping away and fast.

Baby what's wrong?

I haven't been here since my father's funeral

Kevin presenting with a confused look

My father, we we're members here. This was the
only church my father felt comfort in. He was home
here.

With Amanda in his arms Kevin kisses me gently on the lips, takes my hand and leads us inside.

Services just beginning as I hear the first hymn being sung. An usher who I vaguely remember grabs me tightly and whispers "So good to see you. It's been too long. Welcome back.... welcome home. Welcome home both of you". *I smile politely, follow and take a seat in a familiar location, a familiar pew.*

As service continues I scan the congregation of the many faces surprisingly I somewhat remember. *I see childhood friends who now sit with families of their own. I see the old neighborhood bully all grown up and sitting among the deacons. The choir director, an ex-childhood boyfriend of Cynthia's sits proudly. I smile thinking how he was some years back and now serving the lord. I continue making my way through the many faces but avoid making direct contact with the pulpit, looking in all directions but what I need to face, the one place I fear, the last place I saw my father. But my avoidance is short lived. In this moment I look to the pulpit where Derrick stands as the new minister of Queens Village Congregational Church. His words cast over me and a chill sets in.*

Welcome home - welcome home. Amen I am blessed and humble on this Easter Morning Church and I have you and our Heavenly Father to thank.

Amen... *From the congregation*

Over the past few years I've ministered at several churches throughout the south but none of them felt like home. The folks were wonderful but nothing like coming home hallelujah and home amen I am. See God has plans for all of us and his plan for me started over twenty years ago. See my brother from another mother *giggles from the congregation* isn't that what you young people say today? See he and I were tricked into coming to church. *Looking at Kevin* we were told we would meet not just girls but beautiful girls... *Laughing.* That first Sunday you *pointing to Kevin* and I took extra care in getting ready. You would've thought we were the teenage girls. Uncle Paul walked us through those doors and we sat in that pew *pointing to the pew right behind Kevin and I* and in the pew in front of us was a man and his redheaded freckled daughter. *Smiling* See that day - that day I walked in and found my calling. I felt the grace of God - I embodied the grace of God, welcoming him in. Amen. My brother, well he - you became

223

mesmerized by that red headed freckled girl. So from that day we both had a reason for returning every Sunday to the house of the Lord.

As Derrick continues I begin putting the pieces together, can't be... I look over to Kevin who has tears in his eyes. My puzzled look informs him of the confusion of our paths crossing in the past. I return my attention to the pulpit and in mid-sentence Derrick Stops, looks at Kevin and loudly says "It can't be" *all eyes on us! Kevin raises my hand to his mouth and kisses it. He nods and Derrick presents stunned in place. When reality sets back in Derrick addresses the congregation. His voice shivering*

Our God..... Our God... Our heavenly father has a plan for all of us. Plan from the womb on... Church our amazing God has a reason for all things. It may not make sense on the onset but it will at the end. Thank you Jesus. Our God our God. He is all things church. And if I ever had doubt, today of all days I doubt no more hallelujah.

From his words an overwhelming feeling hits. Looking directly in front of me, looking to the place where my father last laid to be viewed, where my father's journey came to an end, six figures appear.

*Standing behind Derrick my father, Rosie, Rosa,
Kevin's parents and Blanche in all their glory
befitting for an Easter Service. I shut my eyes tightly
to make sure what I see is actual. And when I open
my eyes, the images remain and my baby girl looking
straight ahead smiles ever so large. All six sets of
eyes are on us Kevin, my Amanda and me. And as
Derrick looks to both Kevin and me and says once
more* "Welcome home" *a sense of calm comes over
me. With these words spoken one by one the six
images disappear. My father before his exit smiles
larger than I've ever seen and in my ear I hear his
voice* "Sometimes you have to walk through fire to
find yourself and the one you truly love. Often times
that journey brings us back to our starting point. My
baby girl I'm so proud of you. You're the woman I
knew you to be destined to be. Take care of my
beautiful granddaughter and my grandson. Lean on
Kevin he's a strong man, I leave you in good hands.
Beth baby you're finally home. "Welcome Home"
*And instantly sight and sound of my father gone.
Overcome with emotions I begin to weep, falling into
Kevin's arms. Amanda strokes the top my head and*

Kevin the love of my life kisses my hand once again and holds me close.

Amen church.... Amen.... This isn't just my home coming.. God is good. Welcome Home my brother and sister... Welcome home.

Push baby .... Come on...

Kevin I'm tired..

Just one more push..... Come on.... I see the head.

Beth....... Just one more good push ... Come on.

Holding my breath I follow my doctor's instructions and in an instant pain and pressure is replaced with the soft sounds of a cry.

Baby you did it.... You did it...

Beth - Kevin... You have a beautiful baby boy.

Kevin filled with emotion, tears streams down his face.... A son. Baby, my son.

Our new addition is placed on my chest..... I look at his beautiful face and cry uncontrollably.

Baby he's beautiful...

Happy Birthday my baby boy.

You knew it was a boy...

I told you my source..... He ... He's never been wrong.

You two have a name...

I look directly into my husband's eyes meet your son, Kevin Jackson Montgomery Walker Durand!

Elizabeth Cook-Howard

Not the End nor a Beginning

Just Continuing